PARANORMAL COZY

Hearts & Dark Arts

TRIXIE SILVERTALE

Sittin' On A Goldmine
Productions L.L.C.

Sittin' On A Goldmine Productions, L.L.C.

info@sittinonagoldmine.co

www.sittinonagoldmine.co

Publisher's note: This is a work of fiction. Names, characters, places and incidents are products of the author's imagination or are used fictitiously and are not to be construed as real. Any resemblance to actual events, locales, organizations, or persons, living or dead, is entirely coincidental.

ISBN: 978-1-952739-71-2

Cover Design © Sittin' On A Goldmine Productions, L.L.C.

Trixie Silvertale
Hearts and Dark Arts: Paranormal Cozy Mystery : a novel / by
Trixie Silvertale — 1st ed.
[1. Paranormal Cozy Mystery — Fiction. 2. Cozy Mystery —
Fiction. 3. Amateur Sleuths — Fiction. 4. Female Sleuth —
Fiction. 5. Wit and Humor — Fiction.] 1. Title.

CHAPTER 1

HAVE YOU EVER closed your eyes and imagined what your future might be like? I have. There were many times I tried to lessen the sting of life as a foster kid by dreaming about seeing my name in lights. "Mitzy Moon's directorial debut . . ."

Spoiler alert.

Life as a film-school dropout and a practically penniless barista took a shockingly different turn. However, today, as I inch forward in the line of parents picking up students in front of the high school, I can't help but reflect on the way Silas Willoughby changed my entire existence.

What the—?

A tall man in an expensive-looking charcoal trench coat strides by with a perfectly coiffed black chow chow on a golden leash.

Weird. Where was I?

Right. Back in Sedona, Arizona, when I opened my decrepit door to discover a wizened old man hunched in my hallway, time seemed to slow down. His bulbous nose twitched and he harrumphed into his thick grey mustache with, what I can now state with certainty was, disdain.

He had balanced an ancient leather briefcase against the wall and rummaged through the contents while my hangover head pounded and words escaped me. His gnarled hand grasped a bulging manila envelope and he cleared his throat—three times, if memory serves. His saggy cheeks flapped unceremoniously and he announced, "I'm looking for Mizithra Achelois Moon." A gust of pipe smoke and *eau de* denture cream had wafted toward me on the tail of his inquest.

Wait! Is that a mastiff? A plump woman in a red velvet cape is sashaying—true story—past my Jeep with a drooling brindle mastiff on a thick diamond-encrusted chain.

Geez!

Back to my reminiscing about Silas . . . I stared at him in surprise, flavored with a pinch of gut-churning horror. The last time someone had come to the door and slaughtered the pronunciation of my full, legal name, they followed up by informing my babysitter that a commuter train had killed my mother.

I think I nodded; I don't actually remember that part.

He handed me the large envelope and said, "I'm sorry for your loss," before shuffling away.

Hold on a minute! Blonde twin girls with beribboned pigtails and matching Chihuahuas on red leashes? What is going on at this high school?

The current disorientation is similar to the feelings that flooded over me when I looked inside that fateful pouch and found a will, a lot of cash, and a key.

The contents transformed my life—for the better —and filled my heart with love, revealed a secret family, and most of all gave me the gift of gratitude.

And now, thanks to the sometimes cruel/sometimes kind hand of fate, I have the opportunity to push the kindness angle and make a difference in another orphan's life.

The high school student I'm collecting is neither my child nor my actual brother, but, since my father and his new wife recently adopted the boy, I've been making the best of having a stepbrother.

Stellen is a shy, handsome boy who dreams of being a veterinarian. He's still discovering who he is, and his place in the world, but since we stumbled upon the fact that he's the only other person I know who can see ghosts, we have a special bond. He can't communicate with them, like me, but simply knowing that someone else can see them has helped me feel a little less like a freak.

I finally reach the front of the queue, but there's no Stellen.

Lowering the window of my Jeep, I call out to a group of students loitering near the pickup zone. "Hey, any of you seen Stellen Jablonski?"

The girls giggle, and one of the boys calls out, "The woodchuck stuffer?"

Ignoring his reference to Stellen's late father's profession as a taxidermist, I employ my psychic powers to put the wiseacre in his place. "Look, you're already failing geometry, maybe you should avoid failing at life too, and try to be a little less of a jerk. Have you seen him or not?"

The boy's eyes nearly pop out of his head, and the surrounding whispers easily shift to the new hot topic.

"He's in the gym."

"Thank you." And that's what we call manners, kid.

I pull out of line, circle back toward the lot, and park. It's highly out of character for Stellen to be somewhere other than exactly where he's supposed to be. Unlike many of his peers, he's a respectful teenager, with a sense of responsibility and gratitude. If he's in the gymnasium, there's a good reason.

The brisk late-winter temperatures in almost-Canada force me to tug my stocking cap down over my snow-white hair and shove my hands into the pockets of my puffy jacket. Luckily, a petite woman in blue is exiting the building with a rotund basset hound trailing her when I get to the doors, and I'm able to slip inside without exposing my bare hands. My fault for leaving the house without mittens and thinking I'd be safe inside my vehicle.

A huge sandwich board wrapped in repurposed flashing red Christmas lights reads: *Welcome to Cupid's Pet Invention Convention.*

Aha! Things are starting to slide into place. Stellen is obsessed with animals. To further his goal of becoming a veterinarian, he's already working after school as a part-time apprentice at the local animal hospital.

Inside the garishly lit gymnasium, a buzz of untamed activity echoes from the polished wooden floor to the ultra-high ceiling.

A plethora of booths are in an array of readiness. Some are completely constructed, while others are still being unpacked from shipping crates. A handful of interesting inventions are displayed in those that are complete, while many others are only partially constructed and resemble medieval torture devices.

Wandering up and down the aisles, I finally spot my little brother. He's hard at work unpacking the final pieces of a small but intriguing device, and at first I think his cheeks are flushed from the effort. Then I catch sight of *her*.

A tiny, elfin-like creature, with lavender hair, violet eyes, steampunk attire, and a wholly anime vibe. The assortment of buckles, straps, and gears connecting her garments boggles the mind.

"Hey, Stellen, I didn't see you out at the pickup zone."

The color drains from his face. "Oh. Right. Sorry. I— I was— I forgot to text."

Hopefully, my easy laughter will lighten his burden of guilt. "No worries, bro. What's going on here?" I gesture to the contraption beside him.

His cheeks flush a fresh shade of crimson, but it's the cartoon girl who responds.

"Stellen is helping me set up my exhibit. Isn't he just the best? Of course, I could've put it together myself. I built it. But it's, like, super nice to have help. You know?"

My experience with this age range of human has taught me that "you know" is rhetorical, so I stifle a reply.

She continues with barely a breath. "But if he

needs to get home, or whatevs, I can finish by myself."

Stellen's big green eyes plead for assistance.

"Not at all. I'll let Doc Ledo know that you're working the convention floor. I'm sure he can hold things down at the clinic for one afternoon."

He brushes his brown curls back and smiles gratefully. "Um, that's okay. I already texted him."

Kicking out a hip, I plant a fist on my curves and tilt my head. "Oh, I see. So in the order of importance, your own sister falls below the local veterinarian?"

The lavender creature laughs lightly, and I can't help giggling along for the ride.

She bats her beautifully applied false eyelashes and her gaze sparkles. "I'm Yolo. Nice to meet you."

"Nice to meet you. I'm Mitzy Moon, Stellen's stepsister. What's your invention?"

Her energy shifts up a few frequencies, and my psychic senses tingle in anticipation.

"I'm super excited about it. It's a pet aura photography booth. People place their pet inside, and then it takes an aura photo, and I can interpret it for them. It shows a lot about the animal's temperament, but also it can show areas for further investigation—like, medically."

"You have my attention." Smiling, I point to the machine. "How does it work?"

She purses her tiny heart-shaped mouth and gives three rapid whistles. A small dog appears from nowhere, wagging his tightly curled tail.

"This is Bricklin. He's a basenji. He'd be happy to demonstrate." She leans down and places her hands on the knees of her jodhpurs as she coos to the beast in a sugary baby voice. "Wouldn't you like to demonstrate? Wouldn't you? You're such a good boy."

The russet-and-white dog prances into the invention's tunnel like Anubis guiding a soul into the underworld.

Yolo steps forward and draws the thick black curtains closed. Her hands fly over the keys of her laptop and there's a momentary flash of light from within the tunnel.

She pulls back the drapes, and Bricklin struts out as though he himself invented the machine.

"Wait for your reading, Bricklin."

The little pup sits patiently, while both his sharp, pointed ears track every sound in the vast space.

"Step over to my screen, Mitzy. I don't want to waste the photo paper, so I selected 'No Print' for this one."

Smart, friendly, and ecologically aware. What a lovely match for my sweet, strange stepbrother.

She makes room for me in front of the screen,

and I stare at the image. In the photo, the air around Bricklin seems to glow with a variety of colors.

"This yellow band directly around his physical being indicates happiness or satisfaction in his lifestyle. This blue area here shows intelligence and a higher than average aptitude for understanding human communication." Her fingers move to the left side of the image. "These bits of red and purple here indicate his various joys. Purple generally shows a love of outdoor activity, while red indicates a need for closeness and affection. He's just getting over some nastiness from eating a poisoned mouse, so this dark brown streak here on the left side means he's not completely well." She bends and pats Bricklin's head. "A few more days of rest and then back to walkies."

The pup wiggles with suppressed energy and licks her hand.

"That's impressive. Did you build the contraption first and then learn how to interpret the pictures or the other way around?"

She tilts her round face up at me and twists one of the piecey chunks of her lavender hair around her finger as she ponders my question. "Not to be weird, but I've sort of always been able to see auras with the naked eye, but only on animals. I started researching it about four years ago, and that's when I got the idea for the Tunnel of Truth."

I nod my head and give a little whistle. "Great name."

She hops up and bounces on her tiptoes for a moment. "I know, right?"

"I better let you finish setting up your booth." Turning to my utterly entranced brother, I offer him an easy out. "Are you ready to go? Or do you want to text me later when you need a ride?"

His Adam's apple struggles mightily, but he finally forces out a few words. "Can I text you?"

"No problem. I've got a bunch of errands to run, so you just fire off a pickup request, and your personal Uber will be here in five to ten minutes."

He blushes and looks at the floor. "Thanks, Mitzy."

I stride past, pat him firmly on the back, and stop in mid-stride. "Wait, is her name actually Yolo? Like, You Only Live Once?"

He leans toward my shoulder and whispers, "Her full name is Yolonda Olson, but she doesn't like it, so . . ."

Giving him a friendly elbow in the side, I nod. "Hey, let's not forget, you're talking to Mizithra, goddess of Greek cheese. You don't have to tell me about nicknames."

"Nice to meet you, Yolo. Good luck with the convention." I call over my shoulder.

"Thanks, Mitzy. I hope you'll come back during the show. You can bring your cat."

Quite the observant little pixie. The feline hairs on my skinny jeans must've given me away.

"Thanks for the offer, but that would not end well." Waving, I thread my way through the abandoned packing bubbles, carpet remnants, and wads of discarded gaffer's tape with a sly grin on my face.

I believe Stellen has a Valentine's crush.

CHAPTER 2

THERE'S A HINT OF SPRING in the air. Despite the frigid temperatures and the layer of snow still blanketing the ground, the sun has a warmer hue. It's hard to describe when I noticed the phenomenon. Growing up in the Southwest, with sunny days most of the year, I never noticed the way light changes with the seasons. Now that I've spent more than a year as far north as I've ever been, I can see the subtle shifts from grey to hints of yellow, to the deep golds of summer. The bleak winter sun is warming, and I can't wait to ditch all the layers of cold-weather gear needed to keep me alive at this latitude.

Stepping inside the Bell, Book & Candle Bookshop, left to me by my late grandmother, the scent of worlds and possibilities envelops me. Books are truly a gift. Before I can wax poetic and spin dreamily in the dust motes floating down from the tin-plated ceiling, my volunteer employee stomps out of the back room, plants her biker boots directly in my path, and scowls.

"Are you going to tell me what I did wrong, Twiggy? Or do I have to guess?"

She shakes her head and flicks the short bangs of her grey pixie cut to the side. "Believe it or not, doll, you didn't cause this problem."

"Care to share?"

"Since the most recent book theft, I've added some additional security to the Rare Books Loft."

I wish I could tell you that I was able to stop myself from rolling my eyes, but I can't. "Oh brother."

The aptly named Rare Books Loft contains valuable arcane texts, occult tomes, and some one-of-a-kind volumes never translated into English. My grandmother collected the wealth of information with the help of her lawyer and secret alchemist, Silas Willoughby. The same man who delivered the news of my inheritance to Arizona. Prior to our latest theft, a simple chain and a "No Admittance" sign at the bottom of the staircase provided all the security we needed. However, this second robbery has clearly prompted Twiggy to take decisive action.

"Do I even want to know?"

"You tell me, kid. If you trigger the alarm, do you want to know how to shut it off? Or do you want to have to call me and see if I'm feeling generous?"

Shrugging my shoulders, I exhale loudly. "I want to know."

She shoves one hand in the pocket of her dungarees and gestures for me to follow with the other. "That's what I figured. This hook is now fitted with a pressure-sensitive insert. When it's unclipped a thirty-second clock starts ticking, and if the hook isn't replaced within that window, an alarm sounds and automatically sends me a text."

I frown and cross my arms over my chest. "You're serious? You already monitor that chain like a possessed nun at a parochial school. I think the only reason you put in the pressure-sensitive thingy is to double down on enforcing your policies. What if the thief re-hooks the chain behind them?"

She shakes her head. "Come on. No one does that in the middle of a robbery. Only the people who know the rules will hook the chain up properly."

Letting my arms fall limply to my sides, I half-heartedly nod in agreement. "I've gotta say, for a town that shuns technology with as much effort as

Pin Cherry Harbor, it's a rather impressive system. Did you have to fly somebody in from the big city?"

Refusing to answer, she instead unhooks the chain and lets it drop. The clock ticks down, and the ear-splitting alarm shatters the silence.

I cover my ears and shake my head. "All right, all right! I get it. Shut it off."

Twiggy smirks and tilts her head. "Oh, so you *do* want to know how to shut it off?"

With my hands still clasped over my ears, I nod furiously. "Yes! Now, please."

She strides past me and turns into the back room. Next to the ancient computer on our small built-in desk sits a tiny keypad with an LCD screen. Typing in a code, she presses enter, and the horrific cacophony of beeps and sirens ends. She drops onto her rolly office chair, turns toward her computer, and opens the weekly orders document.

"Um, are you going to give me that code?"

She turns slowly in the chair and looks up at me. "You're the psychic. I thought you'd already know."

And this is why I'm so hesitant to tell people about my special gifts. "That's not how it works, and you know it."

Twiggy recites the code and insists that I promise not to write it down. "Commit it to memory, kid. There's no point having a secret code written down where anyone can find it."

"Understood."

Returning to the wrought-iron spiral staircase, I step onto the second tread and hook the chain up behind me as quickly as possible. I still feel rather confident that Twiggy chose this method of security as a way to punish me for all the times I defiantly left this chain unhooked.

The oak reading tables in the Rare Books Loft have been freshly polished, and the brass lamps with their green-glass shades are each carefully aligned in the upper left-hand corner of their respective desks. Before walking across the plush Persian carpets to my apartment's secret door, I turn and lean against the thick curved banister that reaches out in two directions like arms encircling the first floor in a loving embrace.

It's hard to imagine the number of volumes contained within this three-story bookshop, but the architectural decision to leave this lovely mezzanine in place was a solid choice. The light filtering through the 6 x 6 windows creates a cozy, inviting ambience on the first floor and, on the rare occasions when we have customers, I'm sure they appreciate it.

As I approach the candle sconce that serves as the

secret handle to open the sliding bookcase door to my swanky apartment, my heart sinks a little. The book—priceless according to my mentor Silas—that used to sit on the adjacent shelf was stolen during my father's wedding reception. Twiggy had been searching for the new acquisition, *Loca Sine Lumine, Loca Sine Lege*, for years. The book contains cryptic spells and rituals dealing with things like necromancy, séances, and other interactions with the darker side of magic. The title, loosely translated, means "Paths without light, paths without laws." Not the kind of thing that should fall into the wrong hands.

Mr. Willoughby is not a practitioner of magic, and under no circumstances would he refer to himself as a wizard. He is an alchemist and studies the transmutation of matter. However, this missing tome sounds very much like a practitioner's guide to the dark arts.

Pulling the candle handle, I wait for the bookcase to slide open.

Grams rockets out of the closet. "Mitzy! I thought you'd never get back."

The late Myrtle Isadora is not as dead as everyone thinks. Her spirit was tethered to the bookshop, with the help of our resident alchemist, and we've had a riot getting to know each other. Since I'm the only human who can see and hear her, I play a vital role in her afterlife. "What's on your mind, Grams?"

"Where is Erick taking you for Valentine's Day?"

"What?"

She tilts her shimmering head. "Is it a hearing thing, or an understanding thing, sweetie?"

"I heard you. I just— What day is Valentine's Day?"

Ghost-ma throws her ethereal arms in the air. "How can a girl dating a gorgeous, kindhearted man like Sheriff Too-Hot-To-Handle not know that Valentine's Day is next week?"

"Simple. This girl isn't in the habit of being in serious relationships, and, in the past, I've made quite a point of not celebrating the holiday of love. I've been to anti-Valentine's celebrations, I've been to February the thirteenth Galentine's celebrations, and embraced pretty much any and every way one could avoid admitting to being single during this sappy, love-soaked time of the year."

Grams dramatically swishes the silk-and-tulle skirt of her burgundy Marchesa burial gown and clutches at one of her many strands of pearls. "Well, you better get on board! Because Valentine's Day is my favorite holiday, and I'm working on a special outfit for you."

Now it's my turn to throw my arms in the air.

"Why does that not surprise me? Imagine someone with five ex-husbands buying into a holiday based on the fantasy of true love." My sarcastic tone carries more sting than I intend.

Her ghostly eyes sparkle with indignation and she zooms down to eye level. "You listen to me, young lady. True love is not a fantasy. That handsome sheriff of yours is a good-hearted man from the top of his beautiful blond head to the bottom of his, what I'm sure are perfectly shaped, feet."

The reference tickles my funny bone, and I burst into a fit of giggles. "I think you're the only person I know who would describe feet as 'perfectly shaped.' Is that even a thing? Are you losing your ghost mind?"

She swirls up to the ceiling in a fit of ghost fury. "Well, I never!"

"Oh, Myrtle Isadora Johnson Linder Duncan Willamet Rogers, I think we both know that you did. At least five times!"

The familiar gibe dissipates her anger, and she floats down to embrace me. Her ability to take corporeal form, at will, has greatly improved since our first meeting, but there's still a lingering strangeness about the sensation of being wrapped in someone else's energy.

"Ree-ooooow." The furry fiend has returned,

and it sounds like he doesn't have time for gooey emotions.

My half-wild tan caracal appears out of nowhere, as per usual, and his black-tufted ears flick back and forth with irritation.

"Good afternoon, Pyewacket. To what do we owe this pleasure?"

Completely ignoring my attempt at communication, he struts past, brushing my leg with an aloof, accidental hip check, before leaping onto my four-poster bed for his late-afternoon nap. Circling three times, he drops into the down comforter and lays a paw over his eyes, as though he can't bear to be disturbed by our antics.

Fine, two can play the ignore me game. "Oh, did I mention I have some hot gossip?"

Grams swirls toward me, rubbing her phantom hands together eagerly. "Dish!"

"Stellen has a crush!"

She nods and taps a ring-ensconced finger on her coral lip. "Finally! That boy just needs a little boost of confidence. He's handsome, intelligent, and clearly has good taste."

"Are you saying that because he can see you?"

She snickers. "Maybe. Tell me all about the girl, or boy, no judgment."

"It's a girl, and she looks like she stepped straight out of a Japanese anime. She's a lovely, tiny waif, with lavender hair and fantastically complicated clothing."

Grams places a fist on her ample hip and wags her head back and forth. "Now, now, Mitzy. Never underestimate the power of the right amount of junk in the trunk."

I shake my well-stocked caboose in her general direction, and we collapse in a fit of giggles.

"Did you get to talk to her? Is she one of those vapid mean girls?"

"Not at all! She's brilliant. She invented an aura photography machine for pets, and I think she might be a little psychic or something. She also interprets the photographs for the pet owners."

Ghost-ma zooms toward the sleeping Pyewacket and dares to disturb his slumber. "Do you think you could get an aura photograph of Mr. Cuddlekins? Oh, that would be divine!"

"I guess." Chewing my bottom lip, I run through several montages of me attempting to transport a wildcat into a gymnasium full of people and defenseless animals. None of the scenarios ends well. "I'm not sure it would be entirely safe. You know how Pyewacket can be."

She indulgently strokes his head. "Nonsense. He's a perfect angel. Just explain the process to him and I'm sure he'll come along without complaint."

Yeesh! This woman has no better understanding of her spoiled feline in the afterlife than she did when she was alive.

"I heard that."

Holding up my finger, I shake it sternly in her direction. "You know the rules. No thought-dropping. If these lips aren't moving—"

She scoffs and crosses her arms. "You have to give it a shot. Pretty please?"

I kneel next to the bed and proceed to explain the aura photography tunnel, the lovely pixie girl, and Stellen's obsession with both the girl and her technology.

"Reeeee-ow." A warning.

Tilting my head to Grams, I have to disagree with her positive attitude. "That distinctly sounded like a protest. Maybe when the convention is over, she can bring the tunnel here? I'd be happy to pay her for a private photo session."

Myrtle Isadora shakes her head with disappointment.

"Will that meet with your approval, Pye?"

He lowers his eyelids lazily and chooses to pretend I do not exist, rather than deign to reply.

Before Grams and I can get into any additional debate, my phone pings with a text from Stellen. "We'll table this discussion. Looks like it's time for me to go pick up Stellen and see if I can casually invite Yolo to join us for breakfast tomorrow before the convention."

Grams nods and follows me out of the apartment and down the circular staircase. "Good thinking. I like where your head's at. The boy is shy, but he has potential. Just needs a little push in the right direction. And I think you're the girl to give him that push."

There's no need for me to say my "oh brother" out loud; she hears it loud and clear.

The parking lot at the high school is nearly empty by the time I arrive, and I can only imagine that Stellen needlessly strung out the set up in order to spend additional precious moments with Yolo.

There are only a handful of inventors left inside the gymnasium.

"Yolo, do you need a ride too?"

She shakes her head. "Thanks, but no. I drove my Hyundai Tucson here, with all my gear."

"Of course. That makes sense." I nod and smile. "I'm not sure what time you have to get here tomorrow morning to finish setting up, but would you like to have breakfast with Stellen and me at the diner before the convention?"

She shakes her elfin head slowly and blinks her large round eyes before answering. "Normally, I'd say yes, but I'm pretty nervous about the convention. There's a ton of prize money at stake, and I think I'd feel better if I, like, just come straight here in the morning and test my equipment one more time before they open the exhibits to the public, you know?"

Stellen jumps to her rescue. "Yeah, totally. That's a good call. I can bring you something."

Her cheeks flush, and she bats her glorious eyelashes. "That would be sweet. I love cinnamon sticky buns."

He gulps audibly. "Yeah. Also, do I. Cinnamon."

Oh, the poor sweet child. "No problem, Yolo. I'll make sure we're here before they open the doors, and you can enjoy your cinnamon roll after you test the tunnel. Sound good?"

She smiles, winks, and gives three sharp whistles. Bricklin once again appears from nowhere, and the four of us walk out together.

My psychic senses are tingling madly with the nervous anticipation rolling off my stepbrother like the shock waves from an EMP. We part company in the parking lot, and Stellen and I head home.

Pausing in the alleyway between my bookshop and my father's restorative justice foundation, and the penthouse where Stellen now lives, I make one last suggestion. "Did you want to come in and order pizza?"

"I better not. Amaryllis sent a text and said she was keeping a plate of dinner warm for me. I don't want to seem ungrateful."

Placing a hand on his shoulder, I give him a squeeze. "Don't worry, you never seem ungrateful, and I think you're making the right choice. What time do you want to meet for breakfast?"

"The exhibits open at nine, and I'm sure Yolo will be there by seven . . . If we show up by 8:15, that should give her enough time to test her equipment, and enjoy her cinnamon roll, before the crowds swarm in."

"So meet me back here at 7:45?"

His eyes scan back and forth as he does the math. "Will that give us enough time to eat our breakfast and drive to the high school?"

I chuckle as I pull my hand back and head toward the metal alleyway door. "You've seen me eat, right?"

His snicker serves as the only reply as he disappears into my father's building.

Look at me. Not only am I turning out to be an amazing big sister, but I also seem to have a bit of skill in the matchmaking arena.

CHAPTER 3

WALKING IN TO MYRTLE'S DINER, named after
my grandmother and operated by her first husband,
never ceases to provide comfort. A familiar touch-
stone like this is something I never had growing up
in foster care. The idea of dining in a place filled
with people who know and care about me is one of
the many things I've learned to love about Pin
Cherry.

My surrogate grandfather, Odell, offers me his
standard spatula salute through the red-Formica-
trimmed orders-up window, and Stellen and I slide
into our regular booth.

Tally, the best waitress on the shores of our
great lake, shows up with a steaming cup of
coffee for me, and a lovely mug of hot cocoa with
tiny marshmallows for Stellen. "How's every-

thing going over at my big brother's animal hospital?"

Stellen eagerly reaches for the mug of cocoa, but politely replies before gulping it down. "Doc Ledo is the best. I'm not sure how I can ever repay him for all the stuff he's teaching me. It's pretty lit."

Tally nods her tightly bound flame-red bun, but raises an eyebrow in my direction.

"It means great, or cool, or awesome. Something in that vicinity."

My interpretation draws a chuckle from our server, and she shakes her head as she moves on to help other patrons.

"So what's the story with Yolo?"

Stellen's cheeks instantly flush the color of puppy love, and he swallows with difficulty. "I don't know. She's cool, or whatever."

"Do you like her?"

He unwraps his silverware, fumbles the napkin, and drops his fork.

I lean toward him and whisper, "Hey, it's me. You don't have to be nervous. I'm not going to tell her what you say."

My clairsentience picks up on an instant wave of relief washing over him.

"Yeah, sorry. The kids at school—"

"Oh, you don't have to tell me. Kids at school are the worst."

He nods. "Right?"

Before I can pose my question a second time, Odell shows up with a clean fork and slides our breakfasts onto the table. I receive the scrambled eggs with chorizo, the side of golden-brown home fries, and the bottle of Tabasco that serve as my standard delicious breakfast, while Stellen gets the french toast of his dreams.

"Thanks, Odell. You really are a magician back there." I inhale the fabulous aromas.

He nods. "Good to see you two out and about. You headed over to the convention?"

These seemingly prescient comments used to freak me out when I first arrived in town, but now that I'm a "local" I have a grasp of how fast news travels in a small town. "As a matter of fact, we are. We wanted to take a cinnamon sticky bun to-go, for a friend of Stellen's. Can you make that happen?"

The deep creases around his eyes crinkle as he smiles and looks from my full plate to me, and back. "So how much time d'you figure I got? Three minutes?" He raps his knuckles twice on the table and chuckles as he saunters back into the kitchen.

As you can see, my reputation precedes me.

Stellen gulps down a few bites and pauses. "Thanks for not saying girlfriend, or something."

"Hey, I can keep a secret. Plus, I'm a cool big sister. Remember?"

He stops with a forkful of syrupy french toast halfway to his mouth and chokes on his own laughter. "Right. If I do forget, I'm pretty sure you'll remind me."

"Rude."

We share a round of snickers and gobble down our scrumptious morning meal.

While I collect our plates and take them to the dish bin tucked behind the counter, Tally walks over to Stellen with a plastic bag holding a small to-go box.

"I'm not sure if it will stay warm all the way to the high school in this weather, but I warmed it up for you just in case."

"Thank you, ma'am."

Her cheeks nearly match the shade of her hair. "Well, aren't you the sweetest thing?"

He takes the bag, and we hop into the Jeep to deliver his first thoughtful boyfriend gift.

If possible, the gymnasium seems even busier this morning than it was last night. Cupid's entire Pet Invention Convention is buzzing like a massive beehive.

Stellen leads the way to Yolo's booth. But when she catches sight of him, her expression is one of frenzied panic, rather than welcome.

He hurries to her side.

I arrive in time to catch the bagged cinnamon

roll as Stellen tosses it aside and dives into the Tunnel of Truth.

"Can someone catch me up?"

Yolo turns, and her hands gesture frenetically as she speaks. "Everything was fine when I got here this morning. I ran the tests. I even tested the printer. Bricklin was an absolute angel. Like, for reals, it couldn't have gone better."

My assumption is that this story of perfection is not going to end well.

She leans down, and the layered, full bustle on today's deep-purple steampunk overcoat brushes me back a stride. "Can you see it? I'm sure it's the photocathode," she calls to Stellen.

He mumbles a reply from inside the tunnel, but it's not the answer she was looking for.

She stands and runs a finger under each of her eyes while she struggles to blink back tears. "This is unbelievable. I've been working on this invention for, literally, years. And here it is, the most important day of my life, and . . . total meltdown. I could've won, like, thousands of dollars for my invention or school or whatevs. How is this my life right now?"

My suspicion of catastrophe—confirmed. Something's gone wrong with her wonderful invention, and panic has ensued. Time to test little brother's skills. "Hey, Stellen? Can you fix it?"

He slides out with a hopeful glint in his eyes. "I can fix anything. Tools and other stuff would break around my dad's shop all the time, including his truck, and I always figured it out. But Yolo's invention is on the demonstration list for today. I just don't know if I can fix it in time for the judging."

I kneel next to him and fish around in the pocket of my puffy coat. "Tell you what, you take these and all of this." I hand him the keys to the Jeep and a wad of cash. "And I'll see what the Duncan-Moon Philanthropic Foundation can do to influence the judges. Not in a cheating way, just in a 'hey, can we move this invention to tomorrow's list' kind of way."

Yolo grips my arm with surprising firmness for such an airy-looking creature. "Are you serious? You can do that? Oh, my gosh! Oh, my gosh! You're like a fairy godmother! If you can do that, I know Stellen and I can fix it. I built it once, we can rebuild it. Right?"

I get to my feet and pat her on the back as the theme from the Six Million Dollar Man races through my head. *A man barely alive . . . we can rebuild him . . .* "Let's all take a deep breath. Speaking for myself, I function much better when I'm calm and focused. So you two get this thing working, and I'll grease some palms. Again, not in a cheating way."

The sweet little anime waif actually giggles for a moment. "Thank you, Mitzy. Stellen was right about you. You are, legit, the best."

Taking a moment for a mock curtsy, I accept her compliment and stride off to throw my weight, and my cash, around the convention.

The presence of Pin Cherry Harbor's mayor is a solid clue to the whereabouts of the bigwigs. He's surrounded by a handful of brainy-looking men and women dressed in business attire and carrying clipboards. Of course there are clipboards! After all, Pin Cherry Harbor is the town that tech forgot. We have credit card slidey machines, passbooks at the bank, and, with very few exceptions, cash is king at all local establishments.

"Good morning, Mr. Mayor. This looks like a wonderful convention."

The advantage of being one of two people in town with naturally bone-white hair and what I'd like to think are intelligent grey eyes, the mayor instantly recognizes my lineage. "Miss Moon! How good of you to come. Is the Duncan-Moon Foundation sponsoring this event?"

The event promoters and judges immediately turn toward the whiff of money. "Not yet, Mr. Mayor, but that's what I'd like to speak to you about. Do you know who's in charge?"

The mayor slides an arm around my shoulders

as though we're old friends and offers me up to the PIC powers-that-be. "Mr. and Mrs. Cupid, I'd like you to meet Mitzy Moon, founder and president of the Duncan-Moon Philanthropic Foundation. Miss Moon has done some wonderful things for our community, including some invaluable scholarships at this very high school."

Hands are shoved in my direction, and I shake them like the dancing monkey I've become. Fortunately, it's all to support a good cause, and that's reason enough for me. "I was hoping we could discuss a slight change in the schedule. I'm happy to add a Duncan-Moon Foundation prize to the list and cover any expenses that might be incurred as a result of the adjustment."

Lucky for me, I have more than the basic five senses at my disposal. Their initial hesitation vanishes when I offer to foot the bill.

Mrs. Cupid steps forward and smiles, not in a comforting way. It seems like the way Cruella de Vil would've smiled when *101 Dalmatians* were delivered to her creepy mansion.

"Ms. Moon, we will certainly accommodate a schedule shift if we are able. What did you have in mind?"

"I was hoping that we could shift one of the inventors scheduled to demonstrate today over to tomorrow. I know it's a strange request, but if there's an inventor who's scheduled to demonstrate to-morrow and would be willing to trade places, I'd happily compensate them for the irregularity."

She crosses her arms and nods. "I see. Do you have a vested interest in this invention?"

"Oh, absolutely not. Just want to make sure everyone gets the opportunity they came here for."

The hairs on the back of my neck tingle, and I suddenly have a strong dislike for the wife.

"It's rather late in the competition to make those kinds of adjustments, Ms. Moon. Inventors are required to select their day for demonstration when they sign up. There are advantages to being in the first round of judging today, and advantages to participating in the final round tomorrow. It hardly seems fair to force someone to demonstrate ahead of their planned schedule."

Yep. Definitely don't like her.

Mr. Cupid clears his throat and attempts to as-sert his authority. "Well, to be fair, Fiona, if one of tomorrow's scheduled demonstrators would will-ingly swap, there's nothing in the rulebook to specif-ically prohibit such a change."

This guy is on his way to becoming my new best friend. "This is what I'm saying, Mr. Cupid. A com-pletely voluntary trade. And I'm sure the Duncan-Moon Foundation would be more than willing to add a five thousand dollar donation to the top prize."

Fiona's standoffish vibe begins to weaken as her husband grips my hand firmly and thumps me on the back. "Call me Wibb, please. That is quite a generous offer. The current top prize is only three thousand dollars. We wouldn't have time to change the banners, or mention your sponsorship in the radio ads—"

I wave both of my hands in surrender. "Oh no, Wibb, you misunderstand. The Duncan-Moon Foundation doesn't need any publicity from this. In fact, it can be an anonymous donation, if you like. How do we go about finding someone willing to swap places?"

Two of the nameless judges who were orbiting our conversation lean in eagerly.

"Looks like these two might have an idea, Wibb." I keep using his name, like a Tony Robbins acolyte, and point to the eavesdroppers.

He smiles warmly, and his ruddy cheeks tug into a massive grin. "What are you guys thinking?"

The female judge sweeps her bangs to the side. "I heard the man with the reptile display mention that two of his heaters were broken, and he was quite concerned about his exhibits surviving in these cold temperatures. He seemed very upset about having to stay another day, being short on equipment and all."

Wibb pats her so hard on the back her glasses are nearly ejected from her face. She coughs a little, and I link my arm through Wibb's elbow. "Let's go have a talk with that gentleman."

Fiona trails behind us, emitting a mixture of jealousy and suspicion.

I'm not sure what I've done to earn such distrust from her, but this epic performance I'm putting on is not for my benefit. If I can buy another day for Yolo and Stellen, the reward of knowing that I'm the world's best big sister, and an honorary St. Valentine, will be enough.

As we approach the reptile booth, I remember my gut-twisting discomfort around snakes. I want to land on this man's good side, so I better put on a Meryl Streep-level performance.

Wibb takes the lead. "Mr. Thompson? Excuse me, Mr. Thompson, a word?" A small, pale man with a pencil-thin red mustache and wisp of red comb-over approaches with the smooth, silent glide of, dare I say, a serpent.

"Mr. Thompson, we're in a bit of a situation and need to move one of tomorrow's demonstrations to this afternoon. Would you be willing to take an earlier slot?"

Mr. Thompson exhales loudly. "Oh, my prayers

have been answered. I've already lost two heating mats, and this morning a third one went out. I can't combine some of these species, and I'm running out of options. I would love to do my demonstration this afternoon, and if it would be all right, pack up and head for warmer climes as soon as I'm done."

Wibb pats the man heartily on the back. "Absolutely. Good man, Mr. Thompson. We'll put you at the top of the schedule this afternoon, and, as you know, you need not be present to win. You've helped us out of such a bind, my good man."

The snake wrangler is so overjoyed, offering him any additional compensation seems like offering a satisfied diner a second dessert.

Since Wibb doesn't mention my offer of cash, I keep my mouth shut and avert my gaze from the tanks of slithery things. Nod and smile, as my mother taught me.

Wibb scoops me back into the aisle and we march toward a sequestered meeting room. Once inside, Fiona produces a contract more rapidly than a sleight-of-hand magician. "Ms. Moon, if you're serious about making your prize-money donation, we would need to have that in writing, and we would need to speak to the treasurer of your philanthropic foundation."

"Of course. I was absolutely serious. Let me just make a quick call to the treasurer. And I'll sign whatever papers you need." I better wait until after the financial transaction to push my Yolo agenda.

Wibb for the win. "Oh, Miss Moon, who was the inventor we need to move to tomorrow's schedule? The one we're swapping with Mr. Thompson?"

I plaster on a huge smile and pat *him* on the back. "Thank you for keeping us on track, Wibb. The inventor we're rescheduling for Mr. Thompson's slot would be Yolonda Olson."

The snarly expression and aggressive energy rolling off Fiona make me wonder if she's the one who sabotaged the machine.

No time to worry about that; Wibb has already produced his clipboard and made the necessary switcheroo. "There we go. All taken care of, Miss Moon. Thanks again for bringing this matter to our attention and being such a generous supporter of pet inventions."

"It's my pleasure. Now let me just make that quick phone call, and we'll get this paperwork signed."

I'm not looking forward to explaining this most recent act of generosity to my *treasurer*, Silas Willoughby, but the call goes much smoother than expected, and he agrees to deliver a check in the winner's name to the convention the following day.

Fiona seems less pleased than I would've expected, but Wibb is all back pats and attaboys.

Ignoring the scrooge, I extend a warm invitation to my co-conspirator. "Wibb, would you care to accompany me to Miss Olson's booth and give her the good news?" This enormous smile is gonna give me cheek cramps!

He taps his clipboard and broadens his grin. "Wonderful idea. Just wonderful."

CHAPTER 4

BACK AT THE Tunnel of Truth, my amazing news goes over like a lead balloon. To her credit, Yolo puts on a brave face and graciously thanks the event organizers. But, once they shuffle off to attend to other convention business, she collapses cross-legged on the floor and shoves chunks of cinnamon roll into her mouth.

Finally, something I have in common with this rare creature—stress eating. "What's wrong? I thought the extra day would give you the time you needed?"

She looks up, and her huge violet eyes brim with tears. "I can't thank you enough for whatever you did. If we didn't live way past where Jesus lost his sandals, I'm sure that a day would've been enough time. But Stellen and I confirmed it was the photocathode that was damaged. It looks like there are micropipe defects in the silicon carbide wafers."

Her scientific mumbo-jumbo is meaningless to me, but my extrasensory perceptions tell me everything I need to know. "Don't give up hope, all right? Stellen can be surprisingly clever. If he thinks he can fix this thing, I'd put my money on him."

She draws a ragged breath and licks some sticky caramel sauce from her fingers. "I hope you're right. He said he knew a guy that has everything. I just wasn't sure if *everything* included a photocathode though, you know?"

I take a seat on the floor next to her. "Well, it looks like you're stuck with me until Stellen gets back with the part. Is there anything I can do to help?"

She smiles and winks. "Do you know how to prevent pre-avalanche reverse-bias point failures in epitaxially-grown pn junction devices?"

Shaking my head, I raise my hands in surrender. "I don't even know how to spell most of the words you just said. Why don't we take this opportunity to walk around the rest of the convention and check out the competition?"

Her smile wavers and her eyes dart toward the disassembled tunnel. "There's a lotta proprietary stuff here. I'm kind of afraid to leave it unprotected.

You go ahead and walk around. I'll stay here with Bricklin."

I nod my head as though I'm in agreement. "Great plan, except for the fact that I have no idea what qualifies as competition. Let me see if I can call in a favor." Leaving her on the floor to finish her cinnamon roll, I call my boyfriend. "Good morning, Sheriff Harper."

Without missing a beat, he asks me who's dead.

"Hey, I could be calling to make conversation, not to report a crime. You don't know."

His warm laughter makes my skin tingle, and I hope he buys what I'm selling. "Do you have a few minutes to stop by the high school?"

He makes no objection, so I continue.

"Stellen and his friend have an invention on display at this pet expo thingy, and something malfunctioned on it this morning, so they had to disassemble it. She's nervous about leaving her proprietary technology unprotected—"

He jumps to the conclusion before I can complete my sales pitch.

"Well, no. You're right, it's not *technically* a crime scene, but someone could've tampered with it. I was hoping your well-trained eye would be able to put her fears to rest about possible sabotage."

Whether it was my convincing argument or his hidden need to see me, he agrees to come to our collective rescue. Ending the call, I slip the phone in my pocket and mentally pat myself on the back. Still got it, girl.

I distract myself from the anticipation of Erick's arrival by playing a subdued game of fetch with Bricklin.

When Sheriff Harper arrives, I allow my inner film student a slow dolly shot with a push in at the last minute.

Erick's blond locks are slicked in place with his favorite pomade, and he's wearing that uniform like a runway model at Paris Fashion Week. The way his jacket hangs open to reveal that row of buttons leading down—

"Is that him?" Yolo elbows me and nods toward the approaching badge.

I cough to cleverly disguise my open mouth. "Yep. Here comes the law. Wait, who's trailing him?" He has a deputy who barely looks old enough to shave in tow.

Sheriff Harper's warm smile melts my insides. "Mitzy Moon, meet Deputy Candy."

Shaking the man-child's hand, I can't stop myself from blurting, "Candy? Like, C - A - N - D - Y?"

The youthful deputy nods and exhales loudly. "Thanks for not rhyming it with something or making a porn star joke."

His candor catches me off guard, and I have to cover my mouth to keep from hooting with laughter. "You're quick on your feet, Candy. That's going to come in handy—" Gulp. "I didn't mean to make a rhyme. That was totally accidental. It's just— Quick thinking is useful in this town."

Erick chuckles. "Good save, Moon." He gestures to the under-construction machinery behind me. "Is this the invention?"

I jerk a thumb toward Erick and wink at the rookie. "See what I mean. You can learn a lot from this guy."

The deputy nods, but refuses to take the bait. "I've been reading through a lot of the old case files, Miss Moon. Seems like I may be able to learn quite a bit from you as well." An easy grin graces his boyish face.

Is he flirting with me? Was that flirty? Right in front of my boyfriend? Awful brave for a newbie. "Flattery will get you everywhere," I joke, and gesture for Yolo to join me for introductions to the officers. "So, this is her invention. She and Stellen are in the middle of repairing it. Would it be all right if she and I walk the convention floor while you two poke around for potential clues? There's a lot of prize money at stake, so sabotage isn't impossible."

Erick nods.

Yolo squeezes my arm. "Can you tell them not to touch anything?"

"Also, it would be great if you can conduct your investigation without actually moving any of the parts. It's a pretty complicated machine, and they have to get it back together and ready for demonstration by tomorrow's round of the competition."

"10-4," says the new deputy.

Erick leans toward me and whispers, "So basically, you called us over here to serve as private security, while you snoop around for possible sabotage suspects?"

I let out a low whistle and quickly kiss him on the cheek for distractionary purposes. "Nothing gets by you, Sheriff."

I'd like to tell you that I'm hanging on Yolo's every word as we wander down the rows of invention-filled booths, but my mundane sense of hearing is off-line due to the amount of focus I'm pouring into potential psychic signals. That, and I'm madly rubbing the ancient magicked mood ring on my left hand, silently begging for assistance.

"Mitzy? Mitzy, are you in there?"

I stare at the purple-haired being before me and blink. "Oops. What did I miss?"

She puts a delicate hand over her mouth and giggles softly. "Probably, like, everything. We should get back to the booth. Maybe Stellen found the part and needs my help."

"Copy that. I don't want to abuse the sheriff's goodwill."

As we thread our way through the increasingly thick crowds, Yolo delves into my personal life. "Are you really dating the sheriff?"

"Mmhmm."

She bites her bottom lip for a moment. "He's totally hot, but you seem like a rule breaker. From some of the stuff Stellen said."

Note to self: double-check the stories little brother is spreading around town. "I don't think of it as breaking, more of a bending or stretching."

She chokes on her own laughter. "I'm definitely going to use that line next time I get called into Principal Puig's office."

"You should know, the principal and I are old friends. Next time you're in there, just drop my name, and you should leave with no detention and possibly even a pat on the back."

She laughs out loud and struggles to catch her breath.

We round the corner, and she spies Stellen standing in her booth chatting with Erick. "He's back." She takes off like a gazelle across the Serengeti, and I stroll casually behind like the king of the jungle. Mentally, I had to close that analogy loop for myself.

Stellen catches sight of the approaching lavender streak and waves an object as he smiles broadly.

Even non-inventors like me can guess that he found a replacement photocathode. The two super nerds dive into the tunnel and begin work on the critical repair.

Erick turns to his deputy. "Go ahead and make a pass through the convention center. Be obvious, greet folks, and, in general, make your presence known."

"10-4." Deputy Candy marches off with his thumbs hooked behind his Sam brown.

"He looks a little like a kid at Halloween. How old is that guy?"

"If I tell you he had to have his parents sign a waiver so he could enter the academy, will you promise it stays between us?"

I pinch my lips together firmly and my eyes widen.

Erick chuckles. "He graduated from high school when he was fourteen, college at seventeen, and told his parents he wanted to take all of that brain-power into law enforcement."

"So how did he end up in Pin Cherry?"

"He's one of the smartest recruits ever to complete the program. Highest score in history on the written exam. He lacks a little on the physical strength scale, but his real deficit is common sense—life experience. I think they were hoping to put his brain to use, but keep his body safe by placing him in a less densely populated county for a year or two."

"Well, I scored top marks in common sense, so if you want me to break him in, just let me know."

Erick hooks a finger through my belt loop and pulls me alarmingly close in such a public place. His delicious woodsy-citrus scent threatens to end me, and his lips are so close I can feel his breath as he whispers, "And miss out on all the fun we have working cases together?"

My heart is stuttering like a metronome gone wrong, and breathing is a real struggle. "Erick, there are children present."

He steps back and releases his hold on me, but the fire in his eyes is not diminished. "Do you have plans tonight?"

My heart is beating so loudly, I'm sure everyone within a ten-foot radius can hear. "Me, no. Why?" The attempt to keep my tone casual fails completely, as each word I utter goes up nearly an octave.

He flashes me a crooked grin. "Can I take you

out to dinner? Or would you prefer I grab some takeout and we stay *in*?"

"Um, I mean, you know I'm not totally *alone* at the bookshop."

His recent acquisition of the knowledge that I live with a ghost bubbles to the surface and quenches the fire in his eyes. "Can you lock her out of the apartment?"

Laughter erupts from me so abruptly that I have absolutely no control. Once I catch my breath, I wave my hand and shake my head. "You knew my grandmother when she was alive, right?"

He nods.

"Then I think you know exactly how easy it is to tell her what to do."

He sighs. "Well, I can't exactly invite you over to my place."

For those of you who've forgotten, Erick bought his mother a house after he returned from his second tour in Afghanistan. He lives in the house with her. So, technically, he lives with his mom, but only because he is a wonderful son who wants to repay her for all the sacrifices she made as a single mother. "Blerg. We can't go to your place, and we may or may not have otherworldly interruptions at my place. Where does that leave us?"

He shrugs. "Let's take our chances with

Isadora. Maybe you can strike up a deal. I can't afford to buy a love nest on a public servant's salary."

This time the laughter hits me so hard I snort. The mere thought of a love nest sends a flood of tingles washing over my body. I promised myself I would take things slow this time and not repeat the terrible relationship mistakes of my past. But if he keeps suggesting things like love nests . . . my resistance ain't that strong!

Lucky for me, Stellen and his super-genius friend, who is also a girl, interrupt my uncomfortable conversation with cheers and high-fives.

"It's fixed!" Stellen beams with a combination of pride and self-conscious embarrassment.

"Dude, you're a rock star! Where's Bricklin? Let's test this thing out."

Yolo purses her lips and emits the three sharp whistles that call her canine sidekick to the ready. As usual, Bricklin appears beside her, from who knows where, ready for his assignment.

She powers up the equipment, gestures for the dog to enter the tunnel, and pulls the thick curtains closed.

Erick steps closer to me and whispers, "What is this thing?"

"It takes pet aura photos. Then Yolo interprets the photos and helps pet owners get a better understanding of their animals."

He raises one eyebrow and shakes his head. "If you say so."

Yolo's beautiful hands flutter over her keyboard, and there's a brief flash of light behind the black curtain.

She glances toward me and smiles. "Looks like it worked."

I give her a thumbs up and offer a congratulatory smile to my stepbrother.

Yolo returns to the tunnel and slides the curtains open.

A collective gasp rises from those gathered.

Stellen is the first to find his voice. "Where's Bricklin?"

Several heads nod their agreement with the question.

Yolo's violet eyes widen with fear. She struggles to issue the whistle, but no beautiful basenji appears.

Erick turns to me. "Is this part of the demonstration? Is the dog supposed to disappear? Is it kind of like a magic trick?"

I exhale softly. "No, to all of your questions. Something has gone horribly wrong."

He depresses a button on his radio and requests Deputy Candy to return to the booth immediately. Erick turns and pushes back the crowd. "We just need everyone to step back, please. And if you were here during the demonstration, please don't leave. I have a deputy coming over to take your statements."

A variety of questions echo through the crowd.

"What happened?"

"What's that machine supposed to do?"

"Did someone say a dog disappeared?"

I leave Erick to handle crowd control while I step over to the laptop. "Yolo, can you show me the picture that you just took?"

She wipes a tear from the corner of her eye and nods. She clicks open a folder and launches the app to display the saved image.

The dog is not in the photo. But something entirely unnerving is.

"Stellen. Come quick." The hairs on the back of my neck are standing on end.

He hurries to my side, and the instant he sees the image he squeaks with fright.

Yolo turns and looks at both of us. "What? What is it? Bricklin went in there for the photo. Something must've happened when the photocathode was activated. Maybe it's some kind of quantum acceleration?"

Stellen shakes his head slowly and swallows hard. "Yolo, this is gonna sound freaky. Please don't judge. There are two ghosts in the photo. I can see ghosts."

She looks back at the screen and scans for a hint of what Stellen reports.

Gripping his arm, I ask, "Two ghosts? I only see the girl."

He points to the center. "You don't see Bricklin? Right here?"

I shake my head. Apparently, I can't see animal ghosts. Weird. There's a conundrum for Silas. At least Stellen took the paranormal hit square in the chest this time and didn't drag me under the bus with him. When the inevitable screaming starts, I'll have to come up with a cover story for him.

She reaches out and grips Stellen's arm. "For reals? Ghosts? You can actually see spirit forms?"

He nods, and my extrasensory perception feels him bracing for the next heartbreaking blow.

She bounces on her tiptoes. "That is, like, the best thing ever!"

I can only imagine the confused expression gripping my face. She's not going to flip out? She's not going to point at him and yell, "Freak! Freak! Freak!" What is happening?

Stellen's jaw muscles loosen and he chews on a fingernail. "You're not freaked?"

Yolo bites her lip. "I'm a little freaked that Bricklin is a ghost. Is he dead?" Her voice catches and her eyes flood with emotion.

I offer the only consolation I have. "Let's assume the best for now. I'm no expert, but it looks like that ghost stole your dog—somehow. Maybe he's still alive, but trapped."

She shakes her head. "No way. You're telling me a ghost stole my dog. That's a lead, right?" Her big eyes look at me expectantly.

"It absolutely is." What am I saying?

Unable to release her hold on Stellen, she grips me with her other hand. "Does that mean you'll take the case?"

CHAPTER 5

Sheriff Harper radios Deputy Candy to meet him at the cruiser when he finishes taking statements. Then he grabs me by the elbow and leans deliciously close. "The bystanders were making a lot of noise, but I'm pretty sure I heard you say the word 'ghost' more than once. How about we march on outside and you fill me in?"

Swallowing my nerves, I turn to the adorable lovebirds and plaster on a smile. "Hey guys, I'm gonna look into a few things and get back to you as soon as I can. Are you all right if I leave you here?"

Stellen nods, and Yolo grips his arm for support. "We'll be okay. Thanks, Mitzy."

Erick hustles me outside and offers me a seat inside the patrol car. He hops into the driver's seat and cranks the heater. "So what did I just see? Where's that dog?"

Taking a deep breath, I shuffle through snippets of how much I can reveal without risking my sanctum sanctorum. "So, you know how I can see ghosts?"

He nods.

"And how Stellen can see ghosts."

"Yeah, it's uncanny. Not sure I totally believe in ghosts, but what does that have to do with the disappearing dog?"

"When I looked at the photo that Yolo's machine took, I saw the ghost of a girl in the tunnel."

"Are you sure? A lot of these ghost lights in photos turn out to be hoaxes. Maybe her machine just had a glitch."

"It wasn't a blur or a flash. It was a fully formed girl in a poodle skirt and penny loafers wearing a sweater with a huge organza dahlia pinned on the left side. Her hair was light brown and pulled into a high ponytail, tied with a ribbon that matched the flower in her sweater. Oh, and she had a sweet pair of pink cat-eye glasses."

Erick angles away from me and eyes me suspiciously. "I've interviewed a lot of eyewitnesses in my day, Moon. Not one of them has had the ability to recall what they saw with such detail. You only looked at that photograph for a few seconds. How can you be so sure about the description?"

And here we reach my invisible line in the sand. "I have a super good memory. I told you that before. Anyway, when Stellen looked at the picture, he saw a second ghost."

He exhales and rolls his eyes. "If you're about to tell me it's a greaser in a black leather jacket with his thumbs in the air saying 'Hey,' we're done here."

"Not a human ghost. It was Bricklin. It was the ghost of the dog."

Erick leans forward and grabs the steering wheel with both hands. He bounces his forehead on the top of the wheel. "Hold on. You're telling me that a living dog walked into the tunnel and ten seconds later he's a ghost? That's not possible."

"Normally, I'd agree. But we all saw it happen."

He pushes himself back and takes a deep breath. "Well, some of us saw part of it, and some of us saw a whole lot more than others."

The tone of doubt in his voice pricks my protective bubble, and a little pain in my heart makes my chest constrict. "Are you saying you don't believe me?"

His shoulders sag. "Of course I believe you. I just don't believe *it*. I don't buy the whole dog ghost thing. Give me a chance to catch up, Moon." His bewildered smile eases my hurt. "I'm on your side. Just lagging behind the rest of the *Scooby Gang*."

His reference to one of my favorite cartoons brings a much needed round of laughter to the occupants of the patrol car.

Deputy Candy knocks on the window and waves.

The sudden noise intrudes on our moment. "Looks like your new partner is here. I'm gonna check into this, and I'll have to get back to you."

Erick reaches across and gives my hand a squeeze. "Keep me posted, and ask the girl to disable the machine. I don't need any other pets disappearing while you're solving this case."

I return his affectionate grip and smile. "So you're officially calling it a case?"

He shakes his head and shrugs. "I don't know what to call it, Moon. But I'm looking forward to hearing all about it tonight."

A little shiver passes through me that has nothing to do with the temperature outside. "Copy that."

Stepping out of the vehicle, I nod politely to Deputy Candy, and he smiles a little too eagerly and for a little too long.

What is up with that kid? Doesn't he realize he's batting way out of his league? Not that I'm calling myself a straight-up Bo Derek 10, but I'm old enough to be his babysitter!

Once I'm safely inside the Jeep, I put my phone on speaker and call the almighty Silas. "Good morning, Mr. Willoughby. I have some disconcerting news and I'm definitely hoping you have ideas."

"Allow me to favor you with a brief update before you proceed. I just received word from Twiggy that she is off on a road trip to meet with several of her sources regarding the missing volume. It hasn't come up on any of the regular auction sites, but she knows some folks who deal outside the shelf, if you receive my meaning."

"Oh, I do. Can you meet me at the bookshop?"

"How soon?"

"Stellen and I just witnessed an aura photography tunnel take a photo that caused a dog to turn into a ghost. And that dog-ghost was then kidnapped by another, human, ghost. So you tell me."

Silas gasps with uncharacteristic shock. "I shall depart my residence immediately."

To the bookstore!

Hurrying in through the side door, I tempt fate by hopping over the "No Admittance" chain, and serendipity smiles upon me as I land clumsily, but intact, on the other side.

"Grams! Grams, we have an emergency. Get your ghost butt in here."

A burgundy streak rockets through the wall leading from the printing museum into the bookshop. "Did you say emergency?"

"Silas is on his way over, but it's a paranormal brain bender! We're definitely gonna need all the ghost help we can get."

She zips through the wall into the apartment, while I wait for the door to slide open like a civilized person.

"Don't judge what you don't understand, dear."

Taking a single finger, I point meaningfully toward my lips. "Don't comment on what's none of your business, woman."

She shrugs her designer-gown-clad shoulders. "Should I get the murder wall?"

"Yes, but it's not a murder. At least I hope it's not a murder."

Struggling to quell her excitement enough to take corporeal form, Ghost-ma is not making much progress with the rolling corkboard.

"Here, let me help."

Together, we get the board in place, and she hovers near the stack of 3 x 5 cards, pen in hand.

"Like I said, it's not a murder." I catch her up on the strange happenings at the invention convention, and she makes cards for Yolo, Stellen, Wibb, Fiona, and Bricklin.

Before we can delve too deeply into profiling an animal-stealing ghost, Silas arrives.

"Ah, I see you've begun assembling your list of suspects."

I scoff. "Not so much a list of suspects, as a list of people who were around at the time. The only suspect we have is a ghost. And I have no idea how to track her down."

Silas smooths his bushy grey mustache with a thumb and forefinger, and his jowls waggle as he nods his head. "A girl, you say?"

I repeat my description of the ghost, and Grams zooms in. "She sounds like she stepped right off the floor of a sock hop, sweetie. Either it was some kind of dress-up day, or she's been a ghost since the 1950s."

"I'll have Stellen and Yolo check the yearbooks. If she's been a ghost since the 1950s—"

Grams nods her head knowingly. "I've been able to learn several useful things in the short time since my earthly death. Imagine if someone had over seventy years to work on her skills. I'm not surprised she stole that dog. She's probably lonely as all get out!"

"Grams! I hardly think loneliness is a justification for dognapping and possible pet murder."

She checks her manicure and nods dismissively. "Of course, dear, I'm sure you're right."

"If we can't figure this out by tomorrow, Yolo won't be able to demonstrate her device for the competition. She'll lose her chance at all that prize money." I shake my head and sigh. "It really is a brilliant invention. I can't imagine what went wrong."

"Indeed." Silas steeples his fingers and bounces his chin on the tips of his pointers.

I feel a lesson brewing.

"Describe the events of this morning. Do not leave out anything. The subtlest tidbit could be the clue we need."

"You want me to use the psychic recall?"

He continues to bounce his chin methodically.

"All right, but let me call Stellen real quick and get him and Yolo on this yearbook assignment." After relaying the mission details to my stepbrother and confirming that they disabled the machine, I take two deep breaths and clear my mind. As I play through the events of the morning like a video clip, I pause and rewind as needed to give Silas as much detail as possible.

He draws a deep breath and harrumphs as he scans the 3 x 5 cards on the murder wall. "I believe we should add a card for this Deputy Candy you mentioned. I do not yet see his connection to the events you described, but he was at the venue."

"Add him to the board, Grams." I turn to Silas. "If being at the venue makes someone a suspect, there were hundreds of people in the gymnasium. Deputy Candy took statements from everyone that was gathered around the booth at the time, but it would've been simple to slip away unnoticed."

Silas nods. "Precisely."

"What do you mean? Do you think someone stole the dog, snuck it out of a crowded gymnasium, and then magically made ghost images appear in our photograph?"

"I do not." Silas scoffs at the very thought. "However, it seems more than plausible that the equipment could've suffered from malicious tampering, and the saboteur would've had no problem blending into the crowd."

The morning's sequence of events does not seem to fit with his hypothesis, but Silas and his wild theories will have to wait. My phone pings with a text notification. "Hold that thought. Looks like the junior sleuths have an update."

"found photo. 2 creepy. otw."

Silas leans forward and stares at the phone as though it possesses strange powers. "What is it that you are interpreting? It appears to be a hybrid language."

"It's a text." My face cannot hide my shock and

awe. "You speak a dozen languages and converse in Latin like it's normal, and you've never gotten a text?"

"I couldn't say. My mobile device is simply for placing the occasional phone call, when I am unable to properly converse face-to-face."

My eyes roll wildly of their own free will. "Let me see your phone!"

The ridiculous antique he pulls from his pocket nearly gives me a case of the vapors. "How old is that thing?"

"I can't recall. It works perfectly. Why replace it?"

"Remind me to never send you a text."

"I would have assumed that was understood, Mizithra. I prefer to speak to you in person, so that I may benefit from the subtleties of body language. And if that is impossible, the nuances of the human voice carry important information. Why would I have any interest in reading this mutated script from a small impersonal screen?"

"Why indeed." I permit myself a brief and satisfying chuckle before interpreting the message for my mentor. "It's a text from Stellen, and it sounds like he and Yolo not only located the yearbook containing the girl's image, but they've uncovered a creepy back story. If I know Stellen, he's found a way to temporarily borrow the yearbook from the school's library, and the two of them are on their way here to share their findings."

"Very well. I should like to peruse this annual book for myself."

CHAPTER 6

STELLEN'S VOICE CRACKLES eagerly over the inter-com. "Is it all right if I bring Yolo up to the apartment?"

I hop up from the settee and tap the mother-of-pearl inlaid button on the left. "Come on up. Make sure you hook the chain behind you. Trust me, it's a whole *thing*!"

A moment later the bookcase door slides open, and the tiny purple pixie-girl gasps in amazement. "I love it!"

Stellen blushes with pride. "It's lit, right?"

She nods, and her large violet eyes sparkle as they enter the apartment.

"Welcome to headquarters, Yolo. Sit wherever you like. Silas is eager to get his hands on that yearbook. And, on that subject, how did the two of you get into the school library on a weekend?"

Yolo gazes towards Stellen with admiration. "He's super good buddies with the janitor. I guess he goes in on weekends kind of a lot, to, like, study and stuff."

Stellen smiles and shrugs. "It's awesome, being the only one in there. It's less distracting, you know?"

"Good job, little bro. Connections are important in the world of super sleuthing. Where's the goods?"

He slips off his backpack, unzips the main compartment, and retrieves the book.

Silas accepts the yearbook and admires it with the genuine care of a true book lover.

Stellen steps toward the attorney/alchemist and asks, "Do you want me to show you the memorial page?"

The older man gazes up at the boy and his saggy jowls lift in a nostalgic grin. "Would you?"

Stellen flips to the back of the annual and points to a full-page spread.

I step over beside them and immediately recognize the face from the ghost image in the aura pic. The one in the old book is a black-and-white photo, but the horn-rimmed glasses, high ponytail, and similar outfit confirm the identity of our phantom. I read her name aloud. "Irene Tir. It says here she died in 1956 at something called a *Nikdäg*? What the heck is *Nikdäg*?"

Silas opens his mouth to give us one of his fastidious speeches, but Yolo beats him to the draw.

"Oh, it's a super-old-fashioned tradition, from Sweden or something. It's where the girls asked the guys out. There were, like, lists of available guys, and rules. I did a paper on it for my women's studies class last year. I take classes at the community college. I'll have enough credits for an AA by the time I graduate high school."

I open my mouth to respond, but my moment is stolen by another over-eager teen.

"That's how we met. Taking the extra classes and stuff." Stellen smiles down at his own feet.

"Well, you two might be late to the investigation game, but you're hittin' it out of the park so far." I tap my finger on the glossy page. "The dog in the picture with her looks very similar to Bricklin."

Yolo jumps up from her cross-legged spot on the floor. "I know, right? I'm sure it's a basenji. They started importing them to America in the 1940s, so it's totally possible. They can live up to twenty years under the right circumstances." She sniffles softly. "If they're not turned into ghosts." Her voice catches in her throat and she collapses onto the settee with a moan.

"Don't worry, Yolo. We're gonna figure this out. Right, Silas?"

He leans back in the over-stuffed chair and stares at the image of Irene Tir.

"Time is of the essence. The longer the dog's spirit wanders, the more difficult it will be to coax him back." He smooths his mustache with a thumb and forefinger. "We must uncover the cause of this young girl's demise. Mitzy, I believe it's up to you and your sheriff to ascertain if Irene has any living relatives in the area. Perhaps they know the story of this fateful *Nikdäg* night."

"Understood. I'll just run over to the station. You guys are welcome to hang out here. Maybe Stellen can introduce you to Pyewacket. Sound good?"

Stellen smiles. "Can I show her the printing museum too?"

My extrasensory perception easily translates "printing museum" to "Grams." "I suppose. But I hope it goes without saying, that anything that happens in the bookshop, stays in the bookshop." I tilt my head and raise an eyebrow knowingly.

Stellen is no idiot. He knows exactly what the look on my face means. "You got it."

Grabbing my coat, hat, and mittens, I skedaddle down the circular staircase and head to the sheriff's station.

Deputy Baird, also known as Furious Monkeys, is deep into her favorite phone app when I push through the front door and stomp the snow off my shoes. "Is he here?"

Without removing her eyes from the intense game she's playing on her cell, she nods her head toward the crooked wooden gate.

I push through, and, while I'm crossing the bullpen, Deputy Candy appears from the hallway between the sheriff's office and the interrogation rooms. "Hello again, Miss Moon. What brings you into the station?"

He's changed out of his uniform, and his tight T-shirt barely reaches the waistband of his low-slung jeans. I fight the urge to stare and mumble my answer. "Here to see the sheriff."

He grabs a file box from a desk and lifts it high into the air, to slide on top of the bookcase. In-evitably, his tiny T-shirt rides up, exposing his bare midriff.

Yes, I take a peek. Don't worry, he couldn't give Erick a run for his money if he had a thirty-second head start.

He tracks my line of sight and grins.

I inhale sharply and turn the other way.

"I have a few more boxes to put away, but I'll be free for coffee in about ten minutes."

His brazen invitation has me flustered. I'm not

great on my feet when I'm flustered. So I'm going to ignore this whole exchange. Later, when the perfect response comes to mind, I'll log it away for my next encounter with this eighteen-year-old Lothario.

Thankfully, Erick is in his office and smiles when I walk in. "Have a seat, Moon."

"Quick update for you. The gh— What can I call it, so we both know what I'm talking about, but I don't sound insane?"

He leans back in his chair and rubs his left thumb along his jawline. "Let's just refer to it as the person. That should keep you safe, right?"

"Yup. The person in the photo is Irene Tir. She died in 1956, and she had a pet basenji."

He lets out a low whistle. "Impressive. There are a few too many things that line up to call them all coincidences."

"This is what I'm saying." I lean forward and put on my best grin.

He sighs and hangs his head. "Uh oh, here comes the favor."

"You're not wrong." I take a pause and offer him a suggestive wink. "Can you tell me if any of Irene's relatives live in the area? We'd like to find out how she died, and what happened to the dog."

"Let me ask Paulsen."

My mouth opens and my shoulders droop.

He shrugs. "I know, I know, but she knows

everyone. It's the fastest way to the answer you need. Sit tight."

I will not sit tight. I will sit loosely, and I will dislike every part of this solution.

He returns with the short, squat deputy Paulsen trailing him. Her face bears a permanent scowl, and her right hand rests on the grip of her gun. "What business do you have with the Tirs, Moon?"

When in doubt, lie it out. "My stepbrother, Stellen Jablonski, is doing some research and came across a memorial page in an old yearbook. He'd like to interview the family for additional details."

She raises one brow and eyes me suspiciously. "Yeah, the Tirs own a farm outside of Pin Cherry. Property's been in their family since the early 1900s. I think there's a Kevin or a Kent who lives out there now. Might be a great-great-grandson, or nephew. Not sure how much they'd know."

"Well, I appreciate the information. Thanks."

Her scowl softens minutely, but doesn't quite turn into a smile. She nods curtly and returns to wherever Erick found her.

He crosses his arms in that yummy way that makes his biceps bulge. "Anything else I can do for you?"

My cheeks flush and I can't keep from smiling.

"You might want to ask Deputy Candy to stand down."

Erick's face scrunches up in confusion. "Stand down?"

"Yeah. He's coming on *real* strong. The kid does not take a hint."

He laughs a little too hard at my expense. "Look in the mirror, Moon. Can you blame him?"

The light-pink hue on my cheeks turns to a flaming crimson. "Thanks for nothing, Sheriff."

As I brush past him to squeeze out the door, he leans close and whispers, "See you tonight."

Tingles roll down my spine and my tummy goes all warm and gooey. Luckily, I have enough left in the tank to add a little extra wiggle to my waddle as I head out the front door.

Hustling back to the Bell, Book & Candle, I weigh the pros and cons of taking the teens with me to interrogate the Tir family. In the end, I have to admit that the anime-come-to-life Yolo is practically irresistible. If I bring her and Stellen along for the ride, it should soften up the family and help us get the facts we need much quicker. When those big, innocent eyes fill with tears . . . Decision made.

Silas has migrated to the Rare Books Loft and is researching possible explanations for Bricklin's disappearance, and Stellen and Yolo have returned from their tour. I bring the gang up to speed, and Yolo offers to drive out to the farmhouse.

Maybe growing up in almost-Canada makes one a more competent winter driver, but from my vantage point in the back seat, this excursion only serves to fill me with mounting dread. Yolo manages to keep her vehicle on the road, but only by the skin of her teeth. She's definitely driving over the speed limit, and if we hit even a small patch of ice near one of these four-way intersections, her last-minute break-stomp maneuver is going to fail miserably. I can only cross my fingers and hope we don't encounter a semi truck on a perpendicular trajectory.

Stellen seems cool as a cucumber. Either he is a far better actor than me, or he is legitimately UN-terrified.

By the time we reach the Tir farm, my nerves are a disaster and an unwelcome wave of carsickness is swirling in my gut.

Exiting the vehicle as quickly as possible, I plant my feet on terra firma and gulp in the fresh air.

Yolo places a hand on my shoulder. "You should ride in front on the way home. I always get carsick when I'm sitting in back too."

Sure. I'll let her believe that's the reason. "What's the plan? We definitely can't tell them about ghosts or an aura photo machine gone wrong."

Stellen nods. "I think we should say it's for a school project. Maybe something about the history of Pin Cherry High School and remembering students who were taken too soon?" He shrugs his shoulders and looks toward the two of us for approval.

Yolo claps her delicate hands in a way that reminds me of Grams. "Yes. That's perfect. And I can mention the picture because I have a basenji too." She dabs at her eye. "I won't mention that he's missing right now."

"Great. Stick to the script. Nobody tries to be a hero. Get in. Get out. Got it?"

Stellen smirks. "No man left behind, and more stuff like that."

I roll my eyes. "Lead the way, smart aleck."

He chuckles, and the three of us mount the front steps, ring the bell, and cross our collective fingers.

CHAPTER 7

A MAN LOOKING ROUGHLY the same age as my dad opens the door and sizes up our motley crew. He rubs a hand across his thick salt-and-pepper beard, and eyes Yolo and her steampunk wardrobe suspiciously. "We don't support the high school drama club. You have a nice day."

She smiles and lifts on her tippy toes ever so slightly. "Oh, I completely understand. Are you Mr. Tir?"

The man shuffles backward an inch or two and raises his chin. "I'm Kent. Who's asking?"

"Oh, great. I'm Yolo Olson. My friend Stellen and I are writing an article for the school newspaper. Actually, a series of articles featuring students from the history of Pin Cherry Harbor High School—that were taken too soon. We're interviewing families, highlighting important events from each student's past, and trying to raise awareness about the wonderful people who made our school what it is today."

Wow! She's quick on her feet. Some part of her speech connects with him. He nods and scratches his beard thoughtfully. "So what brings you out here?"

"One of our articles features Irene Tir. She died in 1956, but we were hoping you, or someone in your family, might know something about the girl she was before she passed."

He snuffles and shrugs. "My wife's into all that genealogy stuff. Hold on." He turns and shouts down the narrow hallway of the farmhouse. "Monica? Monica, there's some people here about the family history?"

A woman about my height, with faded blonde hair tucked behind her ears, tentatively peeks over her husband's shoulder. "What's this about?"

Yolo repeats her brilliant speech, as Kent disappears into the bowels of the house. Fortunately, Monica takes the bait.

"Oh, I'd love to help you out. I think it's just great that you're working on a school project on the weekend. Come on in and have a seat at the kitchen table. I'll grab my laptop and the photo albums. I can certainly give you any information I have on Irene."

We follow her into the house and take a seat at her large kitchen table. Six old wooden chairs surround a white-legged table with a thick butcher-block top. Every piece of décor in the kitchen is an incarnation of pig. There are little piggy salt-and-pepper shakers, a rotund porcine cookie jar, and various wooden and porcelain versions of swine in chef's hats and/or aprons. This woman has a serious pig preoccupation.

The lady of the house returns with her laptop and three ancient photo albums. She slides a photo book toward each of us and smiles. "You can page through these, while I call up the genealogy information on my computer. I have this great software that tracks everything. I spent years requesting information from family members and making notes and new entries whenever something was submitted. I'm actually really happy you guys showed up today. It's a lot of work, you know? For me it's a hobby, but it's kind of nice for someone to actually want to look at it."

Yolo flashes her an enchanting smile. "I can't tell you how much this means, Mrs. Tir."

Monica blushes a little and glances toward the stove. "Can I offer you some hot chocolate, or maybe you kids drink coffee? I know a lot of kids your age do."

I smile at our hostess. "I think hot chocolate would be fine for all of us. Thank you very much."

"No trouble at all."

She pulls a saucepan from a cupboard and re-trieves milk, baking chocolate, sugar, and several spices. At this point, it dawns on me she is going to make hot cocoa from scratch. Something that never would've occurred to a "packet girl" like me. "Oh gosh, Mrs. Tir, that looks like a lot of work. We're fine with water."

She brushes my comment away with a swipe of her hand. "Nonsense. It takes two minutes. You keep paging through those scrapbooks, and I'll have this ready in a jiffy."

Stellen glances at me and shrugs. I return the gesture and open my album. Yolo is the first to strike it rich. "Look! This is the picture from the memorial page in the yearbook." Her fingers trace over the other photos in the spread, with their edges care-fully tucked into the red corner holders affixed to the black pages of the album. "These are, like, all of Irene. And there's some more of her dog, too."

Monica leaves her pan simmering on the stove and looks over Yolo's shoulder. "Oh, my goodness. Irene! Of course. What a sad story."

Yolo looks up eagerly. "Did you know her?"

Mrs. Tir's eyes widen. "How old do you think I am, dear?"

The purple pixie-girl blushes and bats her perfectly applied false lashes. "I'm so sorry. I didn't really think about it. Of course you didn't."

Monica puts a comforting hand on her shoulder. "Don't feel bad. When I was your age, I could never tell the age of adults. Anyone from thirty to seventy was all the same to me."

We all offer a compensatory chuckle.

Monica returns to the stove to give her concoction a stir and steps back toward the pictures. "I only remember Irene because of that dog. He's buried in the cemetery right next to her."

She has my attention. This story gets more interesting by the minute. "If you don't mind my asking, how did Irene die?"

"Gosh, aside from the infant deaths during the diphtheria outbreak in the early 1900s, hers was the saddest story I ever entered into the genealogy database. She was a sweet young thing, always helping, always making the extra effort. She was on the decoration committee for that year's *Nikdäg*. Do you know what that is?"

Yolo nods. "Yes, ma'am."

Monica smiles at her with motherly admiration. "Well, Irene had a wonderful idea to set up a spring-themed dance in the fall. You know how cold it gets around here in November, so she thought it would lift folks' spirits to dream of spring. She got a local farmer to donate a big batch of baby chicks, and she took it upon herself to dye them all Easter colors and set up a whole beautiful pink barn in the gymnasium. I'm sure it was magical. The black-and-white photos in the yearbook don't do it justice."

I'd love to interrupt and ask her to head in the direction of the point, but we're supposed to be writing the story of Irene's history, and we should consider all these minute details journalistic gold.

Monica presses her hand to her heart. "Well, as you can imagine, baby chicks don't like to be dyed pink, purple, and blue, so she got scratched several times. The doctor's report said a few of those scratches were awful deep. And the thing about baby chicks is that they poop as much as they eat. Pardon my French."

We all make gestures of absolution for Monica's harsh use of the word "poop," and she continues.

"And I'm not sure if you're aware, but their feces carry salmonella. Irene's folks had no idea that she had a compromised immune system. Now, most people can fight off salmonella in a day or two. I'm not saying it's pleasant, but you get over it, you know?"

We all nod.

"Poor little Irene. She didn't make it. She collapsed right in the middle of the gymnasium, under the mirror ball, during the last dance of the evening. The story I heard said she was in the arms of her true love."

Yolo leans forward and whispers, "Was it her dog?"

Monica pats her shoulder. "Oh, you truly are the sweetest. No, some boy or other. But that wasn't the end of the sad story."

Stellen is mesmerized by the tale and asks, "What happened next?"

"She was in the hospital fighting for her life, and at the same time her poor little pup took ill."

"What was wrong with him?"

"Turns out he had been fighting distemper for months. They died on the same day."

Yolo gasps and presses a hand to her mouth.

Stellen shakes his head. "How awful."

Monica shakes her head. "Isn't it just? The family buried the dog next to the girl, and there was a big write-up in the paper about the tragedy, and reminding everyone about the dangers of salmonella. Terrible. Just terrible."

We all nod solemnly.

"Irene was a photographer for the yearbook. She probably took half of the pictures in that 1956 yearbook. Can you imagine? To spend so much time and effort capturing memories for your class, and then you end up as one. Well, it's just the saddest thing."

Stellen and Yolo exchange tender glances, but there's something in the story that causes the mood ring on my left hand to burn with urgency. Looking down, I see a flash of an old camera swirling in the black mists trapped inside the cabochon. "Did you say she was a photographer?"

"Mmhmm." Monica steps over to the stove and pours the hot chocolate into four mugs. She passes them out and joins us at the table.

"Do you know what happened to her camera?" Blowing my cocoa, I take a careful drink of the steaming beverage.

Stellen's eyes lock onto me, and the deep emerald irises shimmer with understanding.

Mrs. Tir casually sips her cocoa, wipes her mouth, and shakes her head. "No idea. I would've loved to have something like that, or even one of her adorable poodle skirts. The girl really had an artistic eye."

My extrasensory perceptions pick up on a swelling panic coming from Stellen's side of the table. "Thank you so much for your time, and the hot chocolate. It was delicious. We really need to be going. Do you know if Irene has any other relatives in the area?"

Monica consults her genealogy chart. "Let's see,

Irene had two sisters and two brothers. Looks like they've all passed. One sister never married, one brother lost two children. Oh, poor man! His wife died in childbirth. The other sister's line moved way, and . . . Well, that just leaves us. Kent had an older brother, but he passed away two years ago, white-water rafting in the Colorado River. One of those bucket list things that ended up kicking the bucket. That's why I always tell Kent he's better off living a smaller life for a longer amount of time than reaching for the stars only to fall and cut his life short."

We all nod, thank her profusely for the information and the refreshments, and hightail it out the front door.

My new seating assignment in the front does little to quell my fears on the drive back to town.

From the back seat, Stellen offers his analysis. "There's got to be some connection to the camera. Right?"

If I turn my head to look back at him, I will most certainly hurl. So I keep my eyes locked on the road ahead as I reply. "Yeah. I've been meaning to ask you: Where did you get that part?"

CHAPTER 8

THE SHORT WINTER days send the sun packing by 4:30 in the afternoon, so we'll have to visit Stellen's tinker tomorrow. According to my stepbrother, the photocathode replacement part came from an "ancient" man who deals exclusively in salvaged parts, and has a huge property south of Pin Cherry on the edge of town.

An icy wind rips across the great lake nestled in our harbor and swirls small tornadoes of snow into the air. Back in Arizona, when the desert winds would whip up the sand in this way, we called them dust devils; or massive ones were called haboobs. I'm sure the Eskimos have a similar name for what we're witnessing, but for now Stellen and I call it "freezing" as we regretfully exit the warm interior of Yolo's car to run for cover.

"I'd invite you over to hang out, but Erick is supposed to bring me dinner and let me sneak a peek at the statements Deputy Candy took from the bystanders today."

Stellen shrugs. "No sweat. I know you guys gotta hook up whenever you can."

"For at least the fiftieth time, we are not *hooking up*. We are casually dating and we'll see where things go."

He smirks and traces a heart shape in the snow. In the center, he draws MM + EH. "According to Amaryllis, the two of you spent, like, a week in Arizona. And one night after she downed her third or fourth glass of wine, she spilled that you shared a hotel room."

"You know what? You can file that under none of your business, buddy. Amaryllis doesn't know what she's talking about, and, plus, that's a whole 'nother story."

Stellen chuckles and flashes his eyebrows. "Oh, I'm sure it is."

"Has anyone ever told you what an annoying brother you are?"

For a moment the mirth drains from his eyes, and he swallows loudly. "Actually, no. I've never had a sister before."

Blerg. This kid knows how to win every conversation. If teasing me about my love life doesn't work, just yank one of my heartstrings until it breaks. "You win!"

Stellen scrunches up his face. "Win what? I'm serious. I don't really know how to be a brother. Do I suck at it?"

Sighing in exasperation, I reach over to give his shoulder a squeeze. "Keep in mind, I have no idea what it's like to have a brother. But, as far as I'm concerned, you're crushing it, dude."

He laughs out loud and we part ways in the alley. He heads into my father's building for a lovely home-cooked meal in the penthouse, and I scurry into the bookshop, hoping Erick will be along shortly with some sustenance.

However, once inside I choose to reheat a mug of leftover coffee in the microwave, and tide myself over with a day-old doughnut.

"You really do have no concept of time, sweetie."

The sudden appearance of Grams results in a little spilling of my coffee and a momentary choking on my stale doughnut. "Grams! We agreed upon the slow, sparkly reentry. You can't just pop into existence and shout things at me. I have a delicate constitution."

This blatant falsehood initiates a burst of shared laughter.

"Why don't you head over to the diner for a proper meal?"

Painting my features in a portrait of innocence, I reply, "About that . . ."

Ghost-ma crosses her bejeweled limbs over her bosom and lifts one brow. "I smell a deal?"

"Nothing gets past you. Erick is bringing over some dinner, and he specifically asks that we have privacy."

She zips down to eye level, and I'm certain that I can hear her non-existent heart beating faster. "Privacy? Really? Is tonight the night?"

"Grams! Not only is it none of your business, but I told you I want to take things slow. Now that he knows about you, I think he simply wanted some assurances that there won't be any eavesdropping or peeping ghosts."

"And what are you offering in return?"

I scan the room as though there's an audience to back me up. "Wow. Are you blackmailing me?"

She shrugs and adjusts one of her many diamond rings.

"Fine. In exchange for your complete and total absence from the apartment until tomorrow morning at 10:00 a.m., I will allow you to pick out a marginally sexy outfit for me to wear this evening."

She rockets up to the ceiling, clapping her hands maniacally. "Give me twenty minutes." She swoops into the closet I call *Sex and the City* meets *Confessions of a Shopaholic,* and her murmurs of glee give me cause for concern.

Meanwhile, I take the opportunity of her preoccupation to have a shower. The thick swirling steam and delicious eucalyptus body scrub clear my head and calm my nerves.

Wrapping one towel around my freshly scrubbed hair and one around my body, I go to work on makeup application. Next, I apply some product to my hair and attempt to use the round bristle brush to blow it out the way Grams taught me. It doesn't turn out great, but it's definitely better than the stocking-hat hair I was sporting pre-shower.

And now, like a lamb to the slaughter, I must join Grams in the closet.

"Do your worst."

She grins and points at the two options she's selected.

My eyes nearly pop out of my head as I scan the items placed on the padded mahogany bench in the center of the space. "You can't be serious?"

She swirls above the 1950s-style cocktail dress, pearls, and slip-on heels with fur trim and shrugs. "Don't blame a ghost for dreaming."

I approach the second option, which consists of a crossover cashmere sweater, black skinny jeans, and suede ankle boots with at least a four-inch heel. "I'll definitely be choosing option number two."

Her shimmering shoulders sag, and she begrudgingly returns the outfit from another era to its proper place in the closet.

"May I have a bit of privacy to get dressed?"

She blasts through the wall of the closet into the apartment. "Make it snappy. I want to get a good look at you before I'm banished."

Her flair for the dramatic never ceases to make me smile. The jeans are quite snug, but I'll chalk that up to the extra treats I snarfed during the holidays. The sweater fits perfectly, even if the neckline is a little plunge-y, and the warm purple hue reminds me of Yolo. The boots are more comfortable than they appear, and by the time I stride out of the closet and perform the requisite spins, I'm feeling pretty good about myself.

"And you should! You look fantastic. That color is divine on you. Erick is a lucky man."

I pantomime pushing her out of the apartment. "He's not going to be that lucky, so don't get your hopes up. I'll see you tomorrow morning at 10:00."

She exhales loudly. "Such a spoilsport." Her laughter lingers even after she disapparates.

BING. BONG. BING.

Let the date night begin! I rush down the stairs and catch the toe of my boot on the "No Admittance" chain as I attempt to climb over. My ankle gives a little, but I save myself from serious injury with a last-minute desperate lunge for the railing.

Twiggy has me terrified to unhook that chain, now that it's set to trigger a secondary alarm. The last thing I need is to launch my evening with Erick to the tune of sirens and bells.

"Who is it?" I ask coyly.

"It's the escort you requested, Miss. The service sent me."

Erick's hearty chuckle radiates through the steel alleyway door, and I push it open with one fist on my hip. "Hilarious."

He opens his mouth to issue a snappy reply, but then his eyes get real busy checking out my ensemble.

"You—that's definitely—nice outfit."

I grab the bag from his hand. "Nice outfit? That's where you landed?"

Turning, I strut into the back room to retrieve plates and utensils.

He follows me and mumbles something salacious under his breath.

"I'm sorry, I didn't quite catch that, Sheriff."

He sidles up next to me and pulls me deliciously close. "Oh, you will. I can promise you that."

My knees get wobbly, and I toy with the idea of calling for otherworldly backup.

"By the way, were you able to strike a deal with Isadora?"

"Mmhmm." I'm afraid that if I open my mouth, the drool will dribble down my chin. Instead, I busy myself collecting plates, forks, and napkins. "Did you want to eat down here, or in the apartment?"

"Here's fine. I brought some wine. We can have it with dinner, or we can drink it during the movie."

"We're watching a movie?"

He blushes and shrugs. "If you want. By the way, did you leave that love note in the snow for me?"

My face must show my utter confusion.

Erick grins. "The 'MM + EH' inside the heart."

I blow a raspberry and shake my head. "You can thank my dastardly little brother for that."

He smiles. "I always liked that kid."

I open the food and set the small bistro table with my mismatched plates and silverware. "Do you mind drinking wine out of water glasses? I used to have a couple of wineglasses, but sometimes the resident recovering-alcoholic ghost takes issue with my stemware choices."

"Not a problem." He loads up a plate with lasagna, roasted Broccolini, and cheesy garlic bread from the local Italian ristorante, Angelo and Vinci's.

Taking the seat opposite, I follow suit and dig into the scrumptious pasta.

Erick wipes his mouth with a paper napkin and eyes my sweater as he finishes swallowing. "That color looks really nice on you."

I wash down my cheesy garlic bread with a glug of Chianti and grin. "Oh, it's the color, is it?" I run my finger along the edge of the deep-V neckline and wink.

He snickers. "Careful, Moon. I'm afraid you might be writing checks you can't cash."

For some reason the reference tickles my funny bone, and I can hardly stop laughing.

"Wow. I didn't think it was that funny." He lifts an eyebrow.

Finally getting myself under control, I take a deep breath and explain. "Before I came to Pin Cherry, not only would that not have been funny, but I would've had no idea what you were talking about. But now that I'm a regular in the town that tech forgot, the idea of checks, in and of themselves, is hilarious."

He leans back and lays his napkin in his lap.

For a moment, I can't help but wish he were wearing one of Deputy Candy's tiny T-shirts.

"Did I lose you for a minute there?"

I shake my head and take another sip of wine to hide my smirk.

"So, before you came here, you never wrote a check? How would you pay your bills?"

"Great questions. To be clear, there were a lot of times I wasn't able to pay my bills, and when I did it was usually at the last minute or after it was already late, with cash at a window across the counter from a scowling middle-aged woman looking at me with sad judgey eyes."

He tilts his head, opens his mouth to speak, rethinks his approach, and starts the whole sequence over. "Let me get this straight, you didn't have a bank account?"

I exhale and hang my head. "I'm not sure I like your tone, Sheriff. But the truth is, there's not much call for a bank account that's simply going to have a zero balance or possibly a series of insufficient funds charges. To be honest, paying for everything in cash when I came to Pin Cherry wasn't that much of a change for me. The difference was, I actually had the cash."

He laughs heartily. "I'm not laughing at you, I promise. I'm sorry to ask, but it's gonna bother me if I don't. Did you take care of your outstanding debts once you got the inheritance?"

"Geez! What do you think? Between my dad and Silas, everything I do has to be above board."

He pushes his empty plate toward the middle of

the table and narrows his gaze. "I don't think that's entirely true."

"Rude, but I suppose you're not wrong." I grab the open bottle of Chianti and strut my stuff up to the apartment.

Erick joins me on the settee and refills my glass.

"If I didn't know better, I'd say you're trying to get me drunk, Mr. Harper."

His cheeks flush an adorable shade of pink, and I can't stop myself from kissing him.

He leans back, clears his throat, and attempts to use his all-business voice. "Did you want to look at those eyewitness statements from the convention?"

I set my tumbler of wine on the coffee table, grip the placket of his button-down shirt, and pull close enough for him to smell the wine on my breath. "Not right now, Your Honor, but I reserve the right to examine that evidence later."

He chuckles and scoops his arms around me.

Canoodling, small talk, and somehow a second bottle of wine keep the evening interesting. To be clear, that second bottle of wine is all me—as in, all in my glass. I'm not sure if I'm keeping demons at bay or trying to weaken my own defenses . . .

As we slide past the witching hour into the wee hours, Erick untangles himself from my arms and takes a deep breath. "My shift actually starts at 0600. Trust me when I tell you I don't want to leave. But it's never good to drive a vehicle or brandish a firearm when I'm sleep deprived."

Snuggling back into his embrace, I wish I had the courage to break my own rules. "Brandish a firearm? You're starting to sound like Paulsen."

He grins and kisses my forehead.

There it is. The official sign that *date night* is over, folks. For what it's worth, I appreciate his commitment to serve and protect, and I'm actually happy not to test my severely inebriated resolve.

"Do you mind if I swing by the station and have a look at those statements later?"

He slides his finger along the neckline of my crossover sweater, and I feel as though my skin is on fire. "We can do anything you want as long as you wear this sweater."

And I'm dead.

Struggling to find enough breath in my lungs to form words, I mumble something like "copy that."

He winks, presses the twisted ivy medallion that activates my sliding bookcase door from inside the apartment, and walks out.

The dim light from my apartment provides the perfect fade-to-black moment, as his excellent exit disappears into the darkness of the bookshop.

The bookcase slides closed, and I collapse onto the settee with a groan.

Before I can make plans to change into my pajamas, or fall into bed fully clothed, Pyewacket climbs onto my midriff and settles in.

"Hey, Mr. Cuddlekins, I'm absolutely not sleeping on this settee. Let me up, and you can hog the bed as usual."

Instead of responding or moving, Pye drops something on my chest.

The foreign object surprises me, and I sit up too rapidly.

My bossy caracal leaps to safety while I examine the item.

"A dog collar? Normally you're ahead of the curve, son. But we already know there's a dog missing. I'll log it into evidence, but I'm not sure you're giving us anything we didn't already know."

"Ree-ow." Soft but condescending.

As I lay the green dog collar on the coffee table, the heart-shaped tag clanks against the wood.

"I'm sure you're right, but I need a huge glass of water and I've got to get some sleep."

The ping of a text and the intrusion of Ghostma tie for first place in what wakes me up.

She whizzes around the room. "There's no sign of Sheriff Harper. What happened? Dish!"

Rubbing the sleep from my eyes, I cradle my

head and reach for my phone. "Hold on, Chuck Woolery, let me see who's texting."

The message is from Stellen. Apparently Yolo has decided to withdraw from the competition, and he's helping her pack up the machine and the rest of her booth. I quickly fire back a "so sorry" and tell him to meet me at the bookshop when they're finished.

Grams places a fist on her curvy hip and chews the inside of her cheek. "Are you going to spill, or am I going to have to haunt you?"

"At least let me have a cup of coffee, woman."

She scoffs and vanishes. I take advantage of the reprieve to use the facilities, grab my thick robe, and stumble down to the coffeemaker.

Once I've poured my liquid alert, I have no more excuses.

"Dish. Now." Her glimmering eyes spark with potential retribution.

"All right. All right." I fill her in on the highlights of the evening, and my difficulty in watching Erick walk away.

She chuckles. "Well, partially difficult. Partially I'm sure it was rather entertaining. That man knows how to fill out a pair of jeans."

"Grams!"

She shrugs. "I'm dead, not buried!"

Despite my lack of sleep, or possibly because of

it, the ghost joke gets me giggling until I'm struggling to breathe. "I better grab a quick breakfast at the diner before Stellen gets here. Seems like we're going to have a pretty full schedule today."

An air of sadness settles over Grams, and she floats lazily through the wall. "I sure do miss Odell."

"And he misses you, Grams. I know how close you were during that last year, before you died. Would you like me to give him a hug that's secretly from you?"

She hurtles back through the wall. "Would you?"

"Anything for you, Isadora."

"World's best granddaughter! I love you, Mitzy."

"I love you too, Grams."

CHAPTER 9

AT THE COZY local diner that serves as my home away from home, I deliver Grams' secret hug to Odell and slide onto the red-vinyl bench seat to enjoy a genuine cup of black gold. Traffic at the diner is surprisingly sparse. The convention attendees must've been up at the crack of dawn to enjoy their morning's repast.

I down my usual breakfast with unusual haste and rush back toward the bookshop as my phone pings with a text from Stellen.

"Here."

You have to hand it to the kid. He does not mince words. We load into the Jeep and he gives me directions to the tinker.

At some point, the route begins to feel familiar, and an unsettling swirl upsets my stomach. There is no helpful image in my mood ring, but as soon as I make the next left turn, my worst fears are realized.

The gypsy's shop—*Ania's Emporium.* If I never visit that store again in my lifetime, it will be too soon.

Stellen points. "See that chain-link fence up ahead on the left?"

"Yep."

"That's the junkyard. He has a bunch of stuff inside an old building in the middle, but if you pull up to the gate and press the intercom, he'll come out and let us in."

I turn my head and slouch down in my seat as we drive past the emporium, just in case Ania Karina Nowak is peeking out her front window, giving me the evil eye.

"Why are you acting so sketchy?"

Busted. "It's complicated. The short version is that her and Grams had a long-standing rivalry, and I didn't exactly 'heal old wounds' when I came on the scene."

He chuckles. "*It's complicated.* Classic."

Ignoring his attempt to goad me into revealing my secrets, I put down the driver's window and stretch to push the call button on the tinker's intercom.

"Tell him it's Stellen Jablonski. He knows me."

"Copy that."

"Who is it?"

I glance at Stellen and nod my head. "I'm with Stellen Jablonski. He says you know him."

"Sit tight."

Stellen nods. "Here he comes."

The tall, lanky man brings to mind one of those wobbly windsock people you see in front of car dealerships every weekend. His limbs seem to flail in uncooperative directions as he ambles toward us.

He tugs the flaps of his deer-stalker hat down and spits into the muddy snow as he flips the chain off the gate and swings it open.

Back in Arizona, they call that a cowboy lock. It means that the gate isn't actually locked, it just appears so to the uninformed "non-*vaquero*" passersby.

He waves me through and points confusingly.

Thankfully, Stellen interprets. "Drive straight ahead and park in front of the 'No Parking' sign."

Raising my eyebrows, I tilt my head comically. "Are you serious right now?"

He shrugs. "It's an inside joke with regulars. Trust me. Park by the sign."

I do as I'm told and, as we climb out of the Jeep, Stellen whispers, "Let me do the talking."

Stifling a chuckle, I follow orders.

"What can I do ya for, Jawbone Junior?"

Oh, I'm going to get some mileage out of that nickname later.

Stellen offers his hand, and he and the tinker exchange a friendly greeting. "The other day you did me a real big favor by finding that photocathode."

The tinker nods and rubs the wiry grey stubble on his chin. "Ain't got another one, if that's what you're after."

Stellen laughs amiably. "No. One was enough. Thing is, I was wondering if you knew where it came from?"

The old-timer's milky eyes scan through the dim corners of his memory, and his tongue works between the crevices of his teeth as he searches for the requested information. "Seems to me that was all part of a whole lot I scooped up from the high school about twenty years ago. Maybe more."

"Was it a bunch of cameras?"

The old man smiles and smacks Stellen on the shoulder. "You always were a sharp cookie. Now that you mention it, I reckon it was maybe forty years ago. Bunch of old cameras; even some old rolls of film. Course the film was all ruined, but some of them cameras was in decent shape."

Stellen smiles and nods. "I bet they were. You wouldn't happen to have the camera that gave us that donor part, would you?"

The friendly old man instantly shifts to shrewd business owner. "I might, I might. What's she worth to you?" He lifts his chin and squints.

It takes every ounce of the self-control I don't possess to keep from blurting out an outrageous number.

Stellen is a far better negotiator. "I was thinking you might part with it for a ten spot."

"Pshaw. I'd be a fool to take less than fifty."

My little brother scoffs and shakes his head. "Fifty? I already paid you twenty-five for the photo-cathode. We both know that was the only valuable part in the whole thing. I'll give you fifteen for the camera."

A proud grin turns up one side of the man's wrinkled face and he slips an arm around Stellen's shoulders as we move indoors to complete the transaction.

The tinker disappears into a back room and, after at least five minutes of shuffling, banging, colorful language, and one serious sounding crash, he returns empty-handed. "Well, doesn't that just beat all. The wife has the camera. I forgot. I was in such a hurry for that thing the other day. I ran over to her place and snatched it out of her camera. Then I sold it to you without a second thought."

When the man says "over to her place," a slow

burn tightens around my ring finger and I know the truth without looking.

Stellen turns to offer me the news, as though I'll be pleased. "Oh, his wife owns the tarot shop next door. Should we run over there and see if she'll sell us the camera?"

The tinker snuffles loudly. "She might, she might not, but you'll hafta wait till she gets back from her sister's."

"How soon will that be?" Stellen's shoulders sag.

"S'pose to be late tomorrow night. You come 'round the day after and see if you can strike a deal."

I smile and nod. Underneath my faceplate, I'm freaking out. The last time Silas and I confronted this woman, things got a little *Mortal Kombat!*

Stellen thanks the tinker and we say our goodbyes.

Once we're back inside the Jeep, I have to let little brother in on my big secret. "I can't get into the details, but I had a bit of a run-in with the gypsy, and there's also the historic feud with Grams. There's no way she'll sell me anything."

The tinker appears beside the vehicle, waving us on impatiently.

"You better drive out of here before he gets the Persuader."

I put the vehicle in gear and drive out of the

gate. "The persuader?"

Stellen grins. "Yeah, that's what he calls his rifle."

"Wow, they're quite the power couple."

Driving past the tarot shop, I park out of sight. "Do you remember what Silas said? The longer we wait, the less likely it is we'll be able to bring Bricklin back to the land of the living."

Stellen nods. "A couple more days won't hurt, though. Right?"

Gripping the steering wheel with both hands, I take a deep breath and battle my conscience.

"What are you waiting for, Mitzy? Shouldn't we get back to the bookshop?"

"I'm going to level with you, pal. I wasn't always an heiress or an upstanding citizen. And don't think for one minute that I'm encouraging you to bend the rules."

He scrunches up his face and shrugs. "What are you talking about?"

"I'm going to go get the camera. Right now. I'll leave some money on the counter, so technically it's not stealing. Technically, it's just some light B&E."

"B and E?"

Sighing, I bend forward and hang my head in shame. "Breaking and entering. You can thank my foster brother Jarrell for teaching me how to pick locks and pockets, and run the occasional grift."

Stellen's eyes widen and he leans back in shock. "You were a criminal?"

"Not exactly. I was a suggestible girl with no parents and a desperate need to fit in. I'm not proud of it."

He grins and leans toward me. "Can you teach me how to pick locks?"

"Geez! This is exactly what I'm talking about. I'm not trying to glorify a life of crime. We need that camera. We need it now. I'm our best chance. You wait here, and if I'm not back in fifteen minutes, call Silas."

I grip the door handle, but the firm hand of my little brother on my right arm prevents my egress. "I'm coming with. You'll need a lookout."

"No way."

He smiles wickedly, and I already dislike the twinkle in his eyes. "Either I'm coming with, or I'm calling Jacob right now." The little extortionist pulls out his phone and twists it tauntingly.

"Fine. But you can absolutely never tell my dad about this."

The thrill of victory turns up the corners of his smart mouth. "Deal."

Pulling the vehicle farther off the road, I turn off the engine and slip the keys in my pocket.

We climb over the mountain of snow at the

edge of the emporium's parking lot and slink along the tree line toward the entrance.

I have my lock pick and tension wrench at the ready by the time we reach the door.

Stellen wisely pulls out his phone and acts as a screen, while I drop to one knee and hastily push the pins to the shear line. Lucky for me it's a simple lock with no anti-picking devices, and the plug easily spins. "We're in."

Before pushing the door open, I issue a warning. "There are some chimes hanging up there. Grab them and make sure they don't go off when we slip in."

He nods and stretches up to silence the tinkling before it starts.

I ease the door closed behind us and exhale. "I'll check the back room, you check behind the counter. What am I looking for?"

"It should be a fairly large camera, probably black, but it could be tan. I never saw it, but from what I know about the types of devices that use those photocathodes, they're big."

"Well, that's something in our favor."

We head our separate directions and begin the hunt.

For some inexplicable reason, the theme song from *Mission Impossible* will not stop running through my head.

When I step through the beaded curtain, and of course there's a beaded curtain, I stand still and attempt to calm my nerves. If I can grab a sliver of focus, my extra senses could come in real handy right about now.

Stellen's quiet searching serves as a backdrop, and I follow my breath in and out until I locate that peaceful spot within.

Reaching out with all of my senses, I search for the camera.

The number of strange tingles unnerves me. There are too many magicked or cursed items in this place to allow my senses to lock onto a single one. However, once before I was able to use my mood ring like a divining rod. Let's see if today is my lucky day.

I hold my right hand above the miniature glass dome and beg for assistance.

Fortunately, my moody ring is feeling generous. As I move my left hand around the back room of the shop, the temperature of the ring shifts. I'm deep into a psychic game of hot or cold.

The intensity of the burning sensation peaks at the precise moment Stellen clacks through the beaded curtain.

"You found it!"

Lucky for me, he thought my weirdly extended

arm was a completely natural gesture. I happen to be pointing right at the thing.

"That's the one? You're sure?"

He flips some levers, opens a panel, tilts the thing in a couple different directions, and nods. "This is it."

"Great. Let's get out of here." We head for the front door, but he grabs my jacket. "You said you'd leave some money."

"Right. Thanks for the reminder."

I step over to the counter next to the register and pull a wad of twenties out of my pocket. "Do you think a hundred dollars is enough?"

Stellen smirks. "It's more than enough for the camera, but I'm not sure it's enough for your guilty conscience."

Dropping the bills, I turn and scowl at him. "You're insufferable. Remember, this never happened."

He shrugs. "As long as you keep up your end of the deal and teach me how to pick locks."

I open my mouth to protest, but a strange wave of foreboding passes over me. "We need to get out of here. Now."

Outside the front door, I grab the back of his jacket. "Wait. Do the phone again."

With some difficulty, he tucks the large camera under his coat and once again screens me.

Pulling out my tools, I reengage the lock. It's not always necessary, but since we're trying to leave the place as we found it, apart from the missing camera and the found cash, I'd hate for someone to actually break in and steal something because I carelessly left the door unlocked.

"Done. Let's go."

We crouch low and hustle along the tree line.

Back in the Jeep, I flick the speakerphone on and call Silas.

"Good morning, Mr. Willoughby. There's been a development."

"Good morning, Mitzy. Is everyone all right?"

"Yeah. We went to that junkyard where Stellen got the photocathode, and it turns out the tinker is the husband of Ania Karina Nowak."

Silas harrumphs. "That is not the best news."

"It gets worse. He actually took the part from a camera she had in her shop."

"That is indeed worse. In all likelihood, the item itself was magicked in some way. Perhaps removing the part from the camera changed the curse, but it will be difficult to ascertain the original intent without that camera."

"And that's why I'm calling. We went into the store and got the camera."

"That seems unwise." Silence hangs between us, and finally Silas breaks it. "It is a mistake to underestimate Mrs. Nowak. A mistake I made once before, and will not make again."

Inhaling sharply, I head toward the truth. "She's out of town for a couple days."

Silas harrumphs. "Who was running her shop?"

"It wasn't exactly open." I glance at Stellen and squeeze my shoulders up toward my ears.

"And how did you obtain the camera?"

"You don't want to know the details. Plausible deniability, and all that."

Stellen tries to help. "She left money on the counter."

I can practically feel my phone frost over from the icy tone of Mr. Willoughby's reply. "The boy was with you? Mizithra Achelois Moon, this is a new low."

"I'm sorry! But we don't have two more days. If we're going to save Bricklin—"

"Trust me when I promise you that this topic is not closed. However, a deadly clock is ticking and my retribution must wait. I shall meet the two of you at the bookshop. We will need the missing part. Is it possible to obtain that piece from your young friend, Mr. Jablonski?"

Stellen blushes. "I'll text her right now. She might still have the machine in the back of her car, but otherwise she can totally take out the part and meet us at Mitzy's."

CHAPTER 10

WHEN I TURN from Main Street onto First Avenue, the presence of my mentor's 1908 Model T parked in front of my bookstore does not bring me comfort. I made a terrible decision. Part of me knew that all along. I deserve whatever detention Silas deems appropriate.

Stellen's phone pings. "It's Yolo. She'll be here in like two minutes. She's got the part."

As we walk up the alleyway toward the door, I offer another apology. "I never should've let you come in that store with me. In the future, when I make bad decisions, I'm going to make them alone. And don't try to blackmail me into including you in my trips to the dark side. Got it, Jawbone Junior?"

He laughs. "I'm not a kid, you know? I'm graduating in four months, and when I'm at college, there's not gonna be anyone but me to make decisions. Maybe I'll screw up sometimes, but that's part of life. Right?"

Pulling the door open, I hold it and usher him inside. "Yes, it is. But learning from other people's bad decisions without having to make them yourself is an even better way to grow up."

His eyes twinkle, and he bites his bottom lip. "So what you're saying is, you can always be a good, *bad* example?"

I struggle to keep a stern threat in my gaze. "Just so you know, you're not too old for a swirly."

"Dude, that's disgusting." He unhooks the chain and marches up the circular staircase—laughing all the way.

As though she has psychic powers of her own, my phone instantly rings with a call from Twiggy. I tap the speaker icon while I race to hook the chain back up. "It's hooked. You said I had thirty seconds. Did the thing call you immediately?"

The sound of her cackle traveling through the phone warms my heart. "It's called coincidence, kid. Get over yourself."

"Hello to you too. To what do I owe this pleasure?"

"Got an update for you and Willoughby. Turns out, my guy didn't have the book. But he had a solid lead. Someone contacted him last week looking for hypothetical pricing information."

The hairs on the back of my neck tingle. "Please tell me it wasn't the gypsy."

Twiggy hoots and hollers. "If I didn't know better, doll, I'd say you're psychic." She guffaws at her own hilarious quip.

"Thanks for the update. I'll let Silas know. When will you be back?"

"You miss me already, eh?"

"Absolutely."

"I'll be back in a couple days. Anything I need to know?"

A sigh escapes. "As far as the bookshop, not a thing. But we might have a paranormal update for you by the time you return. See you soon."

"Back at you."

The line goes dead, and, for a minute, a soft knocking at the alleyway door pulls my attention away from the terrible news.

Before I reach the door, Stellen zips past me, pauses for a moment to catch his breath, and pushes open the door. "Hey. What's up?"

The lavender delight that is Yolo steps lightly across the threshold, bats her eyes, and smiles. "Not much. You got the camera?"

He nods. "Follow me."

Silas waits in the middle of the Rare Books Loft.

He offers me a scathing glance and sets the camera on one of the oak reading tables. "Did you bring the part, Miss Olson?"

She retrieves the item from a pocket in her black frock coat and carefully opens the bubble wrap. "Here it is."

"Good. I shall require peace and quiet. The three of you may wait in the apartment, and I shall inform you of what I discover."

Stellen opens his mouth to speak, but I grip his arm firmly. "Come on, guys. Let's head into the apartment."

The bookcase door slides shut behind us, and Stellen immediately lists off five reasons why he should be helping Silas.

"I hear what you're saying, but he's very particular about how he works."

Stellen tilts his head and squeezes one eye partially closed. "How does a lawyer know so much about old books, old cameras, and disappearing dogs?"

Since I've already crossed the line with Silas once today, I choose my words carefully. "Mr. Willoughby is a conundrum. He is widely read, and apparently remembers everything he's ever perused. He has a lot of useful arcane knowledge. If anyone can figure out what's been done to that camera and if there's a way to reverse it, he's our man."

Yolo glances around the apartment and lunges for the coffee table. She grabs the green dog collar as though it's a life preserver in a stormy sea. "Where did you get this? The last place I saw it was in a storage box in my booth. I have to take it off — had to take it off—Bricklin before we demonstrate the Tunnel of Truth." She looks at me with a mixture of accusation and curiosity. "How did you get this?"

"You'd have to ask Pyewacket. He jumped on my chest and dropped it in the wee hours of the morning. I almost never know where he disappears to, and he seems to be able to come and go from the bookshop as he pleases."

Stellen jumps in. "Pye helps with the investigations. If he brought it to Mitzy, it's important."

She rubs the rough nylon and turns the heart-shaped tag over in her hand. "I'll bring you back, my little yodeler." She kisses the tag and slips the collar into her pocket.

Before he can protest, I shoot Stellen an "easy, buddy" look, and we all stare at the floor.

Yolo shifts her weight and inhales sharply. "Have you, like, got anything to eat?"

A girl after my own heart. "Why don't we head down to Myrtle's? Silas will give me a call when he's finished examining the camera."

She rubs her purple fingernails together with a rapid clickety-clack. "Sure. Sweet."

At the diner, we have time for a full, three-course meal.

Appetizer: malts.

Main course: burgers and fries.

Dessert: pin cherry pie à la mode.

The urge to keep checking my phone produces no results. Stellen busses our dishes, and I leave a huge tip.

The sun is creeping away for the evening as we trudge silently down the chilly street. The sky is clear and the icy wind is fierce, but sparkling stars are already grabbing up the real estate abandoned by their solar nemesis.

"What do you think is taking Mr. Willoughby so long?" Yolo hugs her arms around her tiny middle, making me wish I had offered her an extra jacket before we left the shop.

"He's very meticulous. If it's taking him longer than usual, it's not a bad sign. It means he's double-checking everything, you know?"

She nods, but I can tell she's on the verge of tears. Stopping to fake tie my tennis shoe, I rejoin the trio, but on Stellen's left. I give him a sisterly nudge toward the freezing girl.

He looks at me questioningly and shakes his

head. I pantomime shivering and nod toward Yolo. His eyes widen with fear.

I nod encouragingly and stick out my tongue for good measure.

He finally takes the hint and musters up the courage to slip an arm around her shoulders. "Are you cold?"

She immediately curls into his side and shakes. "Freezing. Thanks for noticing."

His eyes shine, and my heart melts a little. Unfortunately, it took so long for him to catch a clue, we're already at the bookshop.

Opening the door, I let the couple squeeze through in front of me, still entwined.

They continue to the Rare Books Loft, while I secure the door behind us.

"Silas, are you here? We need an update."

The cantankerous old curmudgeon leans over the balcony, harrumphs, and smooths his mustache. "I have checked my calculations thrice."

More than one of the "first floor" occupants stifles a giggle.

He ignores us and continues. "The functionality of this device is most complex. I can assure you Ania Karina Nowak had nothing to do with this. I sense her mother's hand at work. Sadly, the woman is no longer with us, or I may have considered requesting her aid."

"Silas, you're talking in circles. Can we get the dog back or not?"

His jowls sag as he glowers at me from above. "Why don't the three of you join me, and we'll discuss our strategy."

Yolo looks at me questioningly, and I shrug. "That's as close to a yes as we're going to get. Let's go find out what we have to do."

Once we've all pulled chairs up to the table that holds the camera, Silas steeples his fingers and slowly bounces his chin on the tip of his pointers.

Little brother grows impatient, but I narrow my gaze and shake my head firmly in his direction. He shrugs and sighs helplessly.

"It is not a solution I am pondering. I am weighing the consequences of sharing certain details with Miss Olson."

Stellen leans forward and begs her case. "You can trust Yolo. She won't say anything about ghosts, or whatever."

Silas nods slowly. "What I am about to share definitely lands on the side of *whatever*, my young friend. But more than that, there are risks. I am concerned that the young woman's constitution may be challenged."

Yolo leans forward and speaks in her own defense. "If you found even the slightest chance that we can bring Bricklin back, I'll do anything. Even, like, one percent of a sliver of hope is more than I have now. I get that it might not work. I get that I might never see him again. So, if you're going to say that it could all go wrong, and he'll be gone forever . . ."

I glance toward Silas and try to send him a mind picture, like he taught me so many months ago. The first image is of the ghost girl at the high school, the second is the memorial page photo in the yearbook. I'm hoping he understands my belief that the ghost plays some part in safely recovering the dog.

He glances at me, a faint smile curves the corners of his mouth, and he nods. "Very well. Success is not guaranteed, as you rightly assumed. I have reversed the functionality of the camera. The three of you will proceed to the high school this evening. Precisely at midnight, you will begin a séance."

Stellen and Yolo lock eyes. Thankfully, they don't interrupt.

"Mitzy will lead the séance. I will explain the details to her alone. If you are able to bring the ghost-dog into the circle, Stellen will take its photograph." Yolo opens her mouth to speak, but Silas holds up a hand. "Because only he can see the animal's ghost."

She nods and smiles at my brother.

"The key is to ground the spirit in this reality

as soon as it's photographed." He pauses and his eyes drift to a faraway place. "If we had something that belonged to the dog before he was transmuted—"

Yolo can't contain herself. She pulls the collar out of her pocket and drops it on the table. "Will this work?"

"Reow." Can confirm.

Silas gazes at the dog collar, bobs his jowls, and turns toward the intrepid feline. "Robin Pyewacket Goodfellow, do I have you to thank for this trinket?"

Pye nods in a very human way, and slinks over to scratch his back against the alchemist's leg.

"The moment after Stellen takes the photograph will be critical. You must slip the collar around the dog's neck, whether or not he is fully corporeal. It is your only chance. One of one."

A tense quiet settles over us.

"Do you want me to break into the high school?" My voice wavers. On the heels of my earlier unsanctioned break-in, I'm finding it hard to believe that he's about to send me on another.

Stellen interrupts. "I have a key."

Three heads whip pan toward my bro. "You have a key? To your high school? How in the world did you get a key?" My mouth hangs open in awe.

"I'm *really* good friends with the janitor. He had a pet turtle that passed away last year, and I mounted it for him. He was super grateful, and he knows I like to study after hours."

Silas claps his hands together with finality. "Excellent. You two get some rest. You will be up rather late this evening."

Yolo and Stellen hurry off to the apartment, while Silas continues my training. I don't bother to tell him that teenagers don't require "rest" to stay up past midnight. Let him think what he will.

"I'm afraid this hinges quite heavily on you, Mizithra. You must lead the séance, and you must coax the ghost girl out into the open. She may have a great deal of control over the dog's spirit. It will be up to you to sever that control."

"How am I supposed to do that? She's been a ghost for decades. She's the strongest ghost I've ever encountered."

"Perhaps. Perhaps not. You must remain calm and focused during the séance. Use all of your senses to ascertain what ties her to this plane. You must undo that connection by whatever means necessary."

"Whatever means necessary?" My eyes widen and my stomach churns. "Are you saying I'm gonna try to exterminate a ghost?"

"I'm saying no such thing. I merely propose that you pay careful attention to the messages you receive. You must act on them. Stellen and the girl will be responsible for rescuing the animal. Your mission is to help Irene Tir cross over. Once and for all."

A strange chill twists up my spine like an icy snake constricting my vertebrae. "Understood. Now, how do I run a séance?"

CHAPTER 11

THE EMPTY HIGH SCHOOL looms in the silver light of the quarter moon. If you ever imagined that it would be an exciting adventure to poke around a high school after hours, let me disabuse you of that notion. As we approach the back entrance next to the rows of dumpsters, I can't stop the montage of images from *Buffy the Vampire Slayer*. Nothing good ever happens in a high school after dark.

Stellen opens the door and holds it for Yolo and me. He leads us through the glow of exit signs and emergency lights toward the echoes of the empty gymnasium.

Yolo checks her phone. "Ten minutes 'til midnight. What do we do?"

As official director of the séance, it's time for me

to take over. "Stellen, open the compass app on your phone and set up the candles. We need one at each of the cardinal directions. Do you know what that means?"

"North, South, East, West. Got it."

"Yolo, take the canister of salt and pour out a circle inside the candles. But don't complete it. Leave at least a one-foot gap between the start and end points."

She gives me a salute and clicks the heels of her purple brogue boots together.

I carefully remove the camera from my backpack and double-check the settings Silas made me memorize. Everything looks good. Nothing got bumped during transport.

"Do I light the candles yet?" Stellen asks.

"Not yet. We have to wait until midnight."

Yolo completes her partial circle and turns to me. "What do I do with the canister?"

"Place it right next to the opening. I'll sit there. When the dog appears, Stellen takes the picture, you put the collar on, and I close the circle. Everyone clear?"

Yolo tilts her head, and her lavender bangs shimmer silver-pink in the light of the gymnasium's red exit signs. "Don't we have to hold hands during the séance?"

"Apparently that's a myth. Silas says that the candles and the need to reach the spirit are more powerful than any of the other pomp and circumstance."

Stellen steps closer and whispers, "What about Irene?"

"That's the most unpredictable part—and the riskiest. You guys need to grab Bricklin and get out of the circle, before I can pour the rest of the salt and close it. But I have to pour the salt before Irene can follow you out. The timing will be critical." The hairs on the back of my neck tingle at the same time as the mood ring on my left hand forms an icy circle. "She knows we're here."

Yolo shivers, and Stellen clears his throat.

"Let's all step into the circle and take our positions."

"Who's gonna light the candles?" Yolo grips Bricklin's collar with two hands and my psychic senses feel the ripples of fear floating off the young girl.

"You two take your places. Make sure you have the camera ready and the collar. I'll light the candles, take my place, and call the ghosts. Are you guys ready?"

Stellen swallows audibly and nods.

Yolo bobs her head and whispers, "Thank you."

"Don't thank me yet. There's a lot that could go wrong. Let's just stick to the plan and hope for the best. All right?"

They both nod and take their places inside the almost-circle of salt.

I light the candles, beginning with the north and ending with the west, as I was instructed, and take my place inside the circle next to the break in the ring of salt. "We three request access to the spirit world. One among us has lost a friend. Taken too soon. Taken before his time. One among us bears a message. Irene Tir, come forth. Be here now."

The silence is suffocating. I push my fears away and continue the call. "Bricklin Olson, Yolo needs you. Your spirit is not meant to cross over. She needs you to join her here and now, in the circle. We call upon all helpful spirits and guides to share your positive energy to bring these entities into our circle. The circle is safe. The circle is sacred. The circle is here, now."

My mood ring chills with a fresh set of frosty messages, and I glance down to see an image of the dog's collar. "They're coming. Get ready."

Stellen positions the camera and places his finger on the shutter button.

Yolo rubs the collar like a good luck charm.

"Think of Bricklin with all your heart, Yolo. Think how much you miss him. Think how much he means to you and how much you want him back. Call him with your heart. Love is stronger than fear."

She nods, and I can sense the shift in her energy. I can almost see the waves of love emanating from her little purple being.

The fresh-faced girl in the poodle skirt is not pleased with our intrusion. The angry and potent ghost of Irene Tir appears in the doorway of the gymnasium. She's calling to the dog, but using the name of her own dearly departed pet. Bark Hudson.

Stellen whispers. "Bricklin's coming. He's running toward Yolo."

Grabbing the canister of salt, I steel myself for the confrontation. "Get ready. Irene is right behind him. There won't be much time."

Thankfully, Irene is stubborn. She maintains her position in the doorway and continues to call to the dog. I can't see the animal's ghost, but the increased panic in her tone indicates he's not responding to her commands.

The camera flashes.

The dog flickers between this plane and the other in the center of our circle.

Yolo lunges forward and slips the collar over the dog's head and onto his solidifying neck.

Irene races toward us, screaming in fury.

She flies into the circle, bent on destruction.

"Now. Phase 2! Now!" I shout to my cohorts, and tilt the salt can.

Yolo scoops up the barely corporeal dog.

Stellen grabs the camera, and together they leap out of the circle.

I instantly complete the ring of salt and face a furious, trapped apparition.

"Where are you taking my dog? Bring that dog back to me immediately!"

Reaching out with all of my senses, I come up sadly lacking on intel. The fear of otherworldly retribution is severely limiting my abilities.

Her wrathful gaze falls on me. "You can't take my dog. I sacrificed everything to save Bark Hudson. You better bring him back—or else."

Without the aid of extrasensory solutions, I'm going to have to spitball my way out of this ghostly disaster. "Irene, I'm here to help you reunite with Bark Hudson. Tell me what you did for him, tell me how you tried to help him, so I can help you."

Her boiling fury cools a couple of degrees. "I gave that gypsy woman all the bread I earned from babysitting jobs I worked since I was ten years old. And I stole my mother's favorite amber necklace and gave it to her as the rest of the payment. She promised me the camera would save Bark Hudson. She said it would help him cross over before the illness ravaged his little body. She said he'd be here waiting for me."

"But you didn't plan on dying in the hospital from the poisoning, did you?"

Her ghostly image flickers with shock, and a little more of her fury seeps away. "I didn't die from poisoning. I've had my ears bashed with that story for seventy years, and I'd love to give every one of those gossips a knuckle sandwich! Ethol Olufsen gave me the royal shaft, and that's the truth. That hateful paper shaker stole the camera from me at the dance. She wouldn't tell me where it was, and I just— I just couldn't take it. I went up to the catwalk in the theater and I threw myself off." She scoffs loudly. "That whole baby chicks, salmonella malarkey was a story my parents cooked up to make sure their good Catholic girl wouldn't end up in purgatory. Sadly, I landed in this can. Much worse, if you ask me."

"I'm sorry, Irene. That's terrible."

Her self-pity vanishes, and her eyes turn to living flame. "Now gimme back my dog or I'll flip my lid and show you what I've learned."

All I can do is cross my fingers and hope that Stellen is on the same page.

At last! Phantom flames begin to consume the ghost of Irene Tir. He must've gotten the camera to burn.

"Irene. Your time on this side of the veil has come to an end. You're no longer trapped. Bark Hudson is waiting for you on the other side. He died just a few days after you, back in 1956. He's buried next to you in the cemetery. You can cross over. You're free. You can be reunited with him, like you always wanted."

As her resistance and anger turn to acceptance, the flames of energy shift to a golden glow. A beautiful smile transforms Irene's face into the innocent girl from *Nikdäg* night.

And as the last sparkles of her spirit fade from this reality, I swear I can hear the yodeling of her beloved basenji, Bark Hudson.

No matter how many times I witness it, the experience of helping, or forcing, a ghost to cross over never ceases to amaze.

Lying back on the highly polished gymnasium floor, I stare at the ceiling in the flicker of candlelight. What a wild ride!

Some days I'm so caught up in the comfort and familiarity of my new life, I forget where I came from. Tonight was more than a gentle reminder of how far I've come. My family, my growing powers, and the chance to help people/ghosts give me more satisfaction than I could've imagined.

Back in Arizona, party-girl Mitzy kept busy fighting to survive. There was always a knot of fear in my stomach—waiting for the other shoe to drop. The first shoe dropped when I lost my mother, and after that everything else felt like a prelude to more disasters.

I think tonight, here inside the circle of salt, surrounded by candles, I'm letting that go. I might actually be able to embrace the idea that I deserve to have good things happen to me.

Mind. Blown.

"Mitzy! Mitzy, are you okay?"

Stellen skitters to a stop in the doorway of the gymnasium and gasps when he sees my prostrate form.

"Oh my gosh! She's dead!" He sprints forward as I sit up to reassure him. "I'm fine. Sorry, I'm exhausted, and I was a little lost in my own head. But I'm all right."

He breaks through the circle of salt, and a piece of me feels that release. He hits his knees beside me and hugs me so tight I can't breathe.

"Hey, buddy, I need air."

Stellen flops to the floor and supports himself

with one hand. "Sorry. When I thought you— It was just—"

Placing a hand on his shoulder, I stare deep into his tender green eyes. "I get it. You can't lose anyone else."

He nods and swipes the tears from his cheeks.

Yolo appears in the doorway, hugging her basenji and glowing with pure joy. "I can never repay you, Mitzy."

"Don't even think about it. We all played our part. If you guys hadn't executed Phase 2 so effectively, we might not be having this conversation."

Stellen drags his fingers through the salt. "Yeah, let me grab a broom and dustpan. We need to clean this up and get out of here."

"Copy that."

We tidy up the gymnasium and collect our things. When I open the back door to toss the leavings in the trash, I'm met with the sight of a literal dumpster fire. "Wow, that thing is still burning?"

Stellen chuckles. "I used the whole bottle of lighter fluid. I panicked. I just wanted to make sure the camera burned, you know?"

"We better get out of here. There's a real good chance that those flames drew some unwanted attention."

Yolo nods, and her purple eyes shine wide in the moonlight. "Yeah. Me and Bricklin waited over there." She gestures to a snowbank fifty feet away. "The flames were like fifteen or twenty feet in the air!"

A lone siren pierces the crisp night air. "That's our cue. Load up!"

We dive into the Jeep, and I fishtail it out of the icy parking lot.

"Turn left. Turn left, right now!" Stellen shouts out instructions.

I've never driven in a rally race, but I know a good idea when I hear one. I dive down the side street, pull into a driveway—that is not mine—shut off the engine and headlights.

The three of us wait in tense silence as the siren grows near.

Flashing red and blue lights zip past the end of the street and continue on toward the high school.

"Do we wait? Or do we make a break for it?" I whisper to my co-conspirators.

Stellen breathes heavily. "I think we better get out of here. You can take this street down to Maple, and then if you cut across on Jefferson, you'll end up connecting to Gunnison."

I start the Jeep and back out of *someone's* driveway with the lights off. Creeping along the street in the moonlight, I wait until we're a few houses down before I pull the lights on. "Do I even want to know why you're so familiar with the secret back route to the high school?"

He shrugs. "I created a map of Pin Cherry for my sixth-grade project. I just kind of know all the streets, you know?"

I choke on my own laughter. "I absolutely do not know. I can barely manage finding my way to the diner and the patisserie! You know you're kind of amazing, right?"

In the darkness I can't see the blush on his cheeks, but my psychic senses pick up on the embarrassed pride in his energy.

Before I can respond, Yolo pipes up from the back seat. "He really is. I meant to tell you that earlier, Stellen. I'm, like, so glad you came to the convention and helped me set up my booth. I was wondering—"

Stellen clears his throat, and I recognize the nervous signal that means he has something important to say.

"Hold on a minute, Yolo. Were you gonna say something, Stellen?"

He grins and looks at me from the corner of his eye. "Yolo, I was wondering if I could take you to Angelo and Vinci's for Valentine's?"

She giggles in the back seat, and Bricklin yodels supportively. "For sure. That would be, like, so lit."

The buzz of young love warms the inside of the

vehicle faster than my sad little heater ever could. The idea of a Valentine's date with a special someone intrigues. Should I wait and see if Erick has something planned, or should I make a grand gesture of my own?

Decisions, decisions.

CHAPTER 12

WHATEVER ENERGY RESERVES I drew upon to hold the séance and help Irene crossover are severely depleted. When we pull up in front of Yolo's house, I'm barely able to keep my eyes open.

"Hey, after you walk her to the door, will you drive us home?"

Stellen nods. "Sure. Yeah, right."

Lucky for him, I gave him the idea to walk her to the door. I don't think it had actually occurred to the sweet, innocent kid.

He hops out and opens the door for her, and she struggles to climb out of the back seat without releasing her hold on Bricklin. I have a feeling she won't be putting that dog down for a couple of days, at least. If Stellen doesn't watch out, that little pupper might be a third-wheel on their Valentine's date.

He steadies her on the icy sidewalk and helps her up the cement stairs in front of the simple wooden door on the small white ranch-style home.

Before he can muster the courage to kiss her good night, the porch light flips on and a worried mother, followed by an angry father, spill out of the home.

Heated and distressed voices swirl to an increasing volume. I hop out of the Jeep and rush to my brother's aid.

Possibly because of my exhaustion, or more likely due to my unshakable clumsiness, I slip on the ice and go down hard on my backside. Thankfully, I've got plenty of padding.

The upside of my accident is that it silences all parties.

From my vantage point on the ground, I chuckle and call out to the parents. "Please excuse my fantastic entrance. I'm Mitzy Moon, owner of the Bell, Book & Candle Bookshop downtown. We were helping Yolo look for her lost dog, and I'm afraid time got away from us. But the good news is, we found the dog!"

Both concerned parents ask their daughter several questions, and she happily confirms my clever lie while I get to my feet.

As I approach the tense scene on the crowded front stoop, an odd thought pops into my head. In all honesty, it seems a claircognizant message. "Adopted." As I glance back and forth from Yolo's mother to her father, I find no traits in common with their elfin daughter. These are both solid, broad humans of some Nordic or possibly Germanic descent. Their hair is a similar shade of mousy brown, and their eyes are the plain sheen of weak coffee. As I examine the visible effects of their DNA, I can't find a single chromosome appearing on the small lavender-topped human in our midst.

I offer my hand to the father, and he hesitantly reciprocates. "Mitzy Moon, you say?"

"That's right, sir. I'm well acquainted with Sheriff Harper, if you need to check my references. Let me start by apologizing for losing track of time. And I wish I'd thought to have Yolo give you a call or text. That's definitely on me. I hope you won't hold it against the kids." Look at me, being all grown up and taking responsibility.

Yolo pipes up with eager praise. "Honestly, Dad, I never would've found Bricklin without Mitzy. She's literally the best. I mean, things were a straight-up disaster. I wouldn't have had a *ghost* of a chance." Violet eyes dart my way and her lovely lashes offer a secret wink.

Stellen clears his throat and struggles to find his

voice. "My name— I'm Stellen Jablonski. We go to school together."

It doesn't take extrasensory perception to see the instant recognition on the parents' faces. Possibly they read the name in the paper, or maybe heard the ever-present small-town rumors. Either way, they are more than familiar with the story that made Stellen an orphan. In unison, both adults tilt their heads to the side and nod. The mother offers her condolences.

"Well, Stellen and I better be getting home. I'm sure glad we could help find this little guy." I scratch Bricklin's head roughly, and he nips at me playfully. Was there a little glow in his eyes? I must've imagined it. I really am sleep deprived.

Stellen offers me his arm and helps me back to the Jeep, sans catastrophe.

Boy, do I have a story to tell Grams and Silas, late, late tomorrow morning, after a sleep-in and a massive breakfast.

CHAPTER 13

THERE'S SOMETHING YOU should know about me: I'm not a patient person. Despite the exhaustion that threatens to steal my consciousness, sleep can wait a few minutes more.

I should be more shocked that Silas answers his phone on the first ring, at 2:00 in the morning, but I knew he would. I call it psychic privilege, and I'm a huge fan—when it works.

"Good morning, Mr. Willoughby, thank you for taking my call."

"Indeed. I found myself unable to slumber while a trio of inexperienced youths tampered with powers far beyond their comprehension."

"I'd like to say I'm offended, but your assumptions are accurate."

He harrumphs. "And how did you fare?"

Taking a deep breath, I launch into my tale. "So, to summarize, the good news is we got the dog back. The bad news is the Sheriff's Department is going to be looking into an unexplained dumpster fire behind the high school."

The late hour has made my mentor punchy, and a deep belly laugh spills from the speakerphone. "I shall rest easy now. I'm pleased the operation was successful. However, I'm unable to join you for your celebratory brunch. The enchantment placed upon that antique camera requires further examination. I must review my notes and discover what I can of its origins. I offer you my congratulations and bid you a pleasant night's sleep."

"Thanks. That shouldn't be a problem. I'm totally wiped." I drop the phone on the nightstand and collapse into bed.

"I'm so glad you were successful, dear."

A huge yawn stretches my jaw to capacity. "Thanks, Grams. Glad you slipped in at the tail end of the story, to save me having to tell it again. When I get back after brunch, I'll make sure everything's in order before Twiggy strolls in to dress me down for bookshop operation infractions."

Ghost-ma giggles and vanishes through the wall.

Pyewacket exercises his superiority by stepping

over me as though I don't exist. He circles three times and flops onto the thick down comforter.

Despite my penchant for running a bit late, I'm the first to arrive at Myrtle's. Before I finish my first cup of java, Stellen and Yolo arrive together. Today, she's a vision in blue. Midnight blue jodhpurs slip into black riding boots, and her pale-blue shirt peeks out from beneath a bright-blue pseudo-military jacket, complete with red and gold epaulettes. My adopted brother shadows her with a love-struck grin plastered on his sweet face. They slide onto the bench seat opposite me and sit adorably close together.

"Is everything all right with your folks?"

Yolo nods, and the two lavender knots on the top of her head resemble bouncing hot cross buns. They appear messy and casual, just a couple of twisted knots held in place by mother-of-pearl inlaid chopsticks, but they hold secure. "Yeah, my dad called Sheriff Harper first thing this morning. But lucky for us the sheriff said a bunch of nice things about you, and my dad said to tell you thanks for helping me find my dog."

Stellen flashes me a crooked smile, and I hang my head and sigh. "Well, looks like I know where I'll be going after breakfast."

They laugh, and she lifts her mug to make room for the plates Odell slides across the silver-flecked white Formica.

Stellen and I eagerly look at Yolo's plate to see what Odell thought she would enjoy. Her lovely purple eyes gaze up at the cook with admiration. "Toad in the hole! I love it! You even brought me, like, extra butter. How did you know?"

Odell winks, raps his knuckles on the table twice, and returns to the kitchen, leaving a gruff chuckle in his wake.

Conversation comes to a standstill as we power through the tempting fare.

When I come up for air, an odd thought pops up. "Hey, don't you guys have to go to school?"

"My mom wrote me a fake doctor's note." Yolo grins and guzzles down some cocoa.

I nearly choke on my home fries. "Wow. What did you do to earn that sweet deal?"

She shrugs her tiny shoulders and smiles. "My grades crush, I help around the house without being hassled, and she knows I'm putting, like, way more into school than I'm getting out of it. So when I need a mental health 'late-start,' it doesn't take much to convince her."

"Nice. What's your story, bro?"

"Um, I pretty much plagiarized your entire 'save the dog' story and re-published it to the praise of Jacob and Amaryllis. She had no problem calling the school this morning to let them know I'd be running late due to family issues."

Shaking my head, I take a long satisfying sip of my go-go juice. "Things sure are different than when I was in school. Of course, I was a complete juvenile delinquent who barely got passing grades, so that might've been part of the problem."

We share an extended laugh at my expense, and they head off to school while I bus the dishes and prepare for a scolding from Sheriff Harper.

The deputy I nicknamed "Furious Monkeys" is hard at work trying to level up on her favorite game.

"What level are you?"

"242." She risks removing her hand from her phone for a brief moment to gesture me through.

"Congrats." You have to admire her dedication, I guess.

The bullpen is empty, and I must admit I'm happy to avoid running into Deputy Candy.

"Boy, am I glad you showed up." Sheriff Harper looks up from the stack of reports on his desk, and a broad smile spreads across his face, all the way to his enticing, blue-grey eyes.

"Well, that's not the greeting I was expecting." I drop onto one of the well-used wooden chairs opposite his desk and return his gorgeous smile. "Were you really looking for me?" A little blush touches my cheeks, and I feel my tummy flip-flop with anticipation.

He leans forward and nods suggestively. "Oh yeah, I figured if I wanted to get to the bottom of the incident at the high school, I should talk directly to the ringleader." His voice takes a decidedly business-y turn, and his eyes no longer hold me in their thrall.

Attempting a surreptitious swallow, I cross my arms over my middle to prepare for the worst. "Should I know what you're talking about?"

He leans back and laces his fingers behind his head.

I recognize a trap when I see one and struggle to keep my eyes focused straight ahead.

"Maybe, maybe not. But I'd love for you to explain to me why Verna Wilson called dispatch last night at 1:46 a.m. to report a 1990s model Jeep Cherokee parked in her driveway for approximately one minute. And while you're at it, maybe you can give me some indication why I had to alibi the story you told Mr. and Mrs. Olson when they called me this morning."

Gulp. Time to battle my own conscience. This would be one of those moments when the truth could get me into more trouble than a lie, but lies are exactly the sort of thing Erick is tired of hearing out of my mouth.

"If you're struggling to fabricate a story, Moon, I don't want to hear it."

"Understood. Would you be willing to meet me halfway?"

He places his hands on the desk and drums his fingers as he weighs his options. "I don't think I like the sound of that."

"I don't mean halfway to the truth, I mean there are certain things I'm not ready to share. So I'll tell you as much as I can, and let you decide what to do with it. I'd love for you to bury it all under a giant mountain of paperwork—" I teasingly gesture toward his desk "—which is not in short supply."

He chuckles lightly and nods. "Let's give it a whirl. I'm not making any promises, and I'm not granting anyone immunity, but I'll keep an open mind."

"Thank you. That's more than fair." I uncross my arms and try to remember everything I learned from *Lie to Me,* and NOT do any of those things. "Stellen and I felt confident we could communicate with Bricklin's ghost. That's Yolo's dog."

Erick holds up his hand. "That's the little purple girl?"

"Exactly. We figured the best time to do that would be when no one else was at the school. So we headed over there around midnight."

"And how did you get in?"

This is where it gets tricky for me. If I tell him about Stellen's key, I could be getting my brother and the janitor into some serious hot water. Better for me to stretch the truth and take the hit. "I picked the lock. You know I can do that."

He nods but doesn't respond.

"Once we were inside, we tried to have a séance. We just used stuff we've learned from TV shows and cobbled it all together." I'm not about to throw Silas under the bus.

"And did you talk to the dog's ghost?" He leans away and tilts his head.

"This is going to sound crazy, I know, but we did. We convinced him to come back. Once Yolo slipped the collar over his head, he was back on this side. Do you know what I mean?"

He shakes his head. "Let's say I believe this wild story. To be clear, I'm not saying I do, it's a hypothetical. What does any of this have to do with the fire in the dumpster?"

"Well, like I said, we based our plan on TV shows. So we figured we better destroy the photocathode if we wanted to keep Bricklin on this side of the veil."

Erick drags his thumb along his jawline, and I can see the muscles flex. "I watch TV too. If I remember my *Supernatural*, burning items is usually part of releasing a spirit's connection to this world. So what is it you're leaving out, Moon?"

Oops. I had no idea his filmography was so current. "True. The next part is going to sound even stranger, but if you really want to hear it, I guess I can risk it."

He leans forward and narrows his gaze. His eyes say, "I'm the law, do what I say," but his energy is desperate for me to simply trust him with the truth.

"All right, here goes." I tell him the sad tale of Irene Tir and the secret about her suicide.

He leans back and exhales. "These details will be easy enough to confirm. The police report would've included the truth, even if it were suppressed for the family's sake. So you burned the camera to release Irene?"

I open my mouth to question how he knew it was a camera, but the strange shift in his energy stops me in my tracks. Something in his psyche just clicked into place like tumblers in a lock. My mood ring burns, and I glance down in time to see a pile of crumpled twenties on a counter. There's no time to disguise the guilt lingering in my eyes.

Erick's eyes lock onto me like a tractor beam. "The owner of Ania's Emporium called this morning to report a strange theft. She said a vintage camera had been stolen, but the thief left a stack of bills by the register—at least twice what the camera was worth. Do you know anything about that?" There's a layer of accusation under the question, and I know we've come to the place where the rubber meets the road. If I deny this, I can probably kiss my relationship with the handsome Erick Harper goodbye forever.

"Can I possibly get a little immunity on this one?"

He shakes his head. "Depends. What's your side of the story?"

"It's not as bad as you think."

He leans back and crosses his arms over his chest, but there's no joy for me.

Time to face the music. I spill the beans about the tinker, the break-in, the camera, and leaving the money on the counter. I don't mention that Stellen was along for the ride, but I do attempt to toot my own horn by mentioning I locked the door behind me.

Sheriff Harper lets out a long, slow exhale and his hands fall to his lap. "Thanks for that, Moon. You know how important honesty is to me. The owner didn't want to press charges. She just wanted to know who broke into her store; although, it sounded like she already had a good idea. When she called, she was cursing your grandmother's name pretty heavily throughout her complaint."

My shoulders fall and I shake my head. "Yeah, I'm sure this didn't do anything to help their feud."

He taps his thumb on the arm of his chair and stands. "I'll let her know the perpetrator has been issued a warning. And ask her if she wishes to pursue a restraining order."

I look up in shock. "A restraining order? I didn't damage anything or threaten anyone."

He leans forward and places his hands on the desk. "I'm sure you can see why Mrs. Nowak would want you to stay away from her property."

"Copy that."

Scraping myself off the chair, I sulk toward the door.

Erick strides around the desk and catches my elbow.

I turn toward him like a scolded child. Eyes down, shoulders stooped.

He inhales sharply. "The timing on this is gonna suck, but I don't want to be a jerk and wait till the last minute. Do you have any plans for Valentine's Day?"

Gazing up at his inviting grin, I burst with the happiness of Tiny Tim gazing upon the Christmas goose. "No. No plans. I was hoping my boyfriend might consider an outreach date."

Erick chuckles and tilts his head. "Outreach date?"

"Yeah, it's where upstanding citizens try to reach the downtrodden and delinquent, with generous pay-it-forward style gestures."

He laughs and scoops me into his arms. "I'd hardly call it slumming, Moon. If anyone's dating on the wrong side of the tracks, it's the wealthy heiress offering charity to the civil servant."

I stretch up and kiss his soft, full lips. "I'd say we both won the lottery, Sheriff."

"Oh, I didn't mean to interrupt." Deputy Candy doesn't dart away or avert his gaze. Instead, he stares directly at me as he delivers his message to the sheriff. "I finished alphabetizing the witness statements from the convention, Sheriff."

The benefit of my extrasensory perception reveals a disconcerting hunger lurking beneath the young deputy's boyish exterior. Rather than pull away from Erick in embarrassment, I cuddle closer and glare defiantly at the unnerving deputy.

Oblivious to the nonverbal exchange, Erick attempts to extricate himself from our embrace. "Good work, Deputy. Take over for Baird at the front desk. She's due for a break."

"10-4." Deputy Candy smirks at me as he turns and strolls toward the front of the station.

Erick finally disengages and looks down at me. "What was that all about? Normally you're not about the public displays of affection."

"I'm telling you, he gives me the creeps. He's very flirtatious. Didn't you see it?"

He raises his eyebrows and shakes his head. "I'm not saying you're wrong, but could you possibly be reading too much into his friendly nature?"

"Whatever. I'm still suffering from sleep deprivation. I better get back to the bookshop and straighten up before Twiggy gets home."

"Where'd Twiggy head off to?"

Great! Open mouth, insert foot. I can't tell him she's been scouring the seedy underbelly of the black market bookselling industry to uncover a stolen volume of dark magic. "She was on a book trip."

Erick shakes his head. "If you say so. I'll pick you up at seven on Friday."

"Sounds good. Is there a dress code?"

The flames that lick at the corners of his eyes send a swirl of heat through my body. "Additional details will be forthcoming, but you should pack an overnight bag."

Oh dear. There goes my heart.

CHAPTER 14

GRAMS IS GOING TO FLIP! I can hardly get back to the bookshop fast enough. When I tell her that Erick is taking me for an overnight Valentine's get-away . . . I mean, her ghost-head might explode.

Even though I slipped out the side door this morning, the heavy brass key around my neck is begging to be used. I stop in front of the intricately carved wooden door and smile fondly at the detailed vignettes.

Someone's car alarm is going off. I can't believe my ears. I thought we got over those in the 90s.

Pulling the chained key out from under my shirt, I turn over the unique triangle barrel in my hand. The sheer heft of it never ceases to bring a twinkle to my naturally curious eyes.

Inserting the one-of-a-kind key into the lock, I twist it three times—ignore the distracting automobile alarm—and listen to the various sets of tumblers fall into place. A satisfying and heartwarming sound.

As soon as I push the door open a crack, piercing sirens hit my eardrums full force and a nauseous swirl stabs me in the gut like a knife.

Not a car alarm.

"Grams! Grams, where are you?"

No response.

"Pyewacket! Pye, what happened?"

No reply.

The stress sends my heart racing, and my breathing comes in shallow gasps. I have to get a hold of myself. I have to calm down and shut off this stupid alarm.

Rushing to the back room, I type in the code. The ensuing silence nearly breaks my heart.

Slipping the key back around my neck, I press both hands to my chest, take slow, deep breaths, and reach out with all my psychic senses.

A montage of unsavory images steals my breath and slaps me across the face like a scorned Victorian woman in *Jane Eyre*.

Steadying myself on the railing, I swallow hard and race up the circular staircase.

There, on the floor beneath the candle handle and my copy of *Saducismus Triumphatus*, lies the motionless Pyewacket.

I surge forward and drop to my knees next to him. He's breathing, but barely. His front paws are covered in blood, and there's something clenched in his jaw.

"Pyewacket, sweetie. Are you in there?"

His eyelids crack open, and his large golden eyes seek out my face. The weakest sound I've ever heard whispers from his mouth. "Reow." Can confirm.

My first instinct is to call Stellen, but he's at school and the best thing for me to do is get Pye to the animal hospital. Stat. "I'm gonna get a towel, Mr. Cuddlekins. I need to take you to see Doc Ledo."

Pyewacket groans, in a decidedly argumentative way.

"Look, I have to take you to the hospital. What could possibly be more important than your life?"

Before he can find the strength to answer, the mood ring on my left hand burns like fire.

I pull the ring into view as an image of the lost red book shimmers in and out of existence. "*Loca Sine Lumine, Loca Sine Lege.*"

The furry mess whines.

"Someone was here? The person who stole the book?"

Pye opens his mouth, but he's too weak to respond. I carefully extricate the tattered shred of fabric from his mouth. And as I rub it between my fingers, the gypsy's name tastes like vinegar on my tongue.

Ania Karina Nowak!

"I knew it." I carefully stroke his head. "Can you wait just another minute while I make sure Grams is all right?"

He groans a second time. This one holds the sorrow of loss. All the pain of the banshee's cry, but none of its malice.

I push away the messages struggling to get through. But in the end it's all too much, and I collapse onto the floor in a pile of tears. My hands shake as I pull my phone into view.

Four missed calls from Twiggy? She's probably on her way to the bookshop to wring my neck.

Great day to forget to turn your ringer on, Mitzy! I hang my head in shame as I hit speakerphone and call my mentor.

"Good morning, Mitzy. I have discovered some alarming details in the layered enchantment used on that old camera."

I open my mouth to share the terrible news, but the only thing that comes out is a horror-filled sob.

"Mizithra, what has occurred? I'm making haste to my car now. What do you need?"

I gasp a ragged breath and choke out the news. "The gypsy— Grams— Pyewacket's hurt."

The terrifying silence on the other end of the phone does nothing to boost my confidence. "You must take Pyewacket to see Doc Ledo at once. I'm on my way to the bookshop, and I will ascertain what Ania Karina Nowak has done with your grandmother."

Attempting to mumble my thanks only brings a fresh set of tears. I slip the phone in my pocket and run into the apartment for a towel.

Carefully wrapping the limp form of my favorite fiendish feline, I shamble to the Jeep like a zombie.

Speed limits are exceeded. Stop signs barely acknowledged.

Fortunately, Doc Ledo is at the front desk when I burst through the door of the animal hospital. He glances at my face and the bundle in my arms and wheels toward me. "Breathing or not breathing?"

"Breathing, but I think he's unconscious. There's so much blood."

"Follow me." He spins in his wheelchair and zooms toward one of the surgical suites.

I place Pyewacket on the table, and Doc Ledo immediately begins his examination.

"Nothing is broken, at least no compound fractures. We'll run a set of x-rays to make sure there are no hairline fractures."

"That seems good, right?"

"That is absolutely good. I'm also not finding any open wounds. Is it possible this isn't his blood?"

The moment Ledo says "blood" I know beyond a shadow of a doubt that Pyewacket got his claws into that gypsy. "It's probably the attacker's. Can you take some samples for DNA testing? I need to pass it on to the sheriff when I report the break-in."

The doctor nods affirmatively and grabs his supplies. He takes careful swabs from each of Pyewacket's front paws and removes some additional fibers, which appear to be human hairs. He packages and labels each piece of evidence with meticulous notations.

"You wait here, Mitzy. I'm going to grab a technician to assist with the x-rays and then we'll get an IV started. My initial examination confirms that there are no physical injuries. He may have been knocked unconscious, as you guessed, and that would explain his grogginess."

Doc Ledo rolls out of the room, and I lean close to Pyewacket. "I know it was the gypsy. Did she hurt you with some kind of magic?"

A fraction of his strength has returned, but his

response is not as cavalier as I'd like. "Reow." Can confirm.

"And Grams? Did she do something to Isadora?"

If caracals can cry, then those have to be tears leaking from Pyewacket's eyes.

It's the only response I need. That horrible gypsy woman has done something to my grandmother, and I'm not going to rest until she pays. Dearly.

Ledo insists that I leave Pyewacket at the clinic for observation. It pains me to be away from him so soon after his injury, but I have to get back to the bookshop and see what Silas has uncovered.

"Silas? Silas, are you in the loft?"

"Indeed." He offers no further information or invitation.

Stumbling up the stairs, I collapse into a chair and let my head drop onto one of the reading tables. "How bad is it?"

He walks to my side and rubs my back with gentle reassurance. "I have never kept things from you, Mizithra. I will tell you everything I know."

My heart sinks and my gut twists in turmoil.

The comfort ceases, and he draws a chair up next to me. "Your grandmother's ghost is gone."

An aching sob rips from my dry throat.

He leans forward and touches my arm. "From what I have deduced, the gypsy has placed your grandmother's ghost in a soul trap. That correlates with the disconcerting information I uncovered as I examined the layers of enchantments placed upon that old camera. Where Ania Karina's mother chose to use her gifts for good, it seems the daughter has been driven to a darker side of the magical arts. If she uncovered her mother's grimoire and, as I suspect, is the individual responsible for the disappearance of *Loca Sine Lumine, Loca Sine Lege,* then she would've had more than enough information to create such a trap."

It takes all of my strength to peel my head away from the desk and wipe my tears. "Is Grams still on this side of the veil?"

"I believe she is. I believe the gypsy trapped her in some type of gemstone or amulet. My forensic magic skills are not as strong as they once were, but I can assure you there was a great battle. Your grandmother did not go without a fight, and her fearless feline protector nearly sacrificed another of his own lives to protect her."

"That blood on his paws has to be the gypsy's. And the piece of fabric in his mouth must be from whatever she was wearing. Doc Ledo collected all the samples, and I can take them to Erick and file a complaint. Kidnapping is a felony, right?"

Silas smooths his bushy mustache with his thumb and forefinger. "I regret to inform you the Penal Code does not carry a punishment for ghost-napping."

Leaning back in my chair, I let my head fall backward as I moan. "Breaking and entering? Animal cruelty? She did something awful to Pyewacket. Something unnatural. The doc said he didn't have any broken bones or open wounds, but he's completely listless and weak."

As I sit up, Silas nods. "You may pursue the punishable offenses with your sheriff. The return of your grandmother's ghost must be left up to me."

The hairs on my arms lift as a chilling wave of power rolls off the alchemist.

"I'm going with you."

Silas rises to his full height, and I shudder in the shadow of his strength. "You shall not. You must remain here and do exactly as I say. I will return to my home, complete my research, and keep you abreast of my plans. Under no circumstances will you accompany me to my confrontation with Ania Karina."

"All right." I choke on my breath a little and feel a wave of weeping clutching at my throat.

"Don't waste your energy on despair. Love is

the strongest magic of all. You must stay here, speak your grandmother's name, and keep her memory alive. It is the loss of those who remember us that strips our souls of their connection. If there is any hope of reaching your grandmother's heart, we must not let the darkness win."

Slowly getting to my feet, I step forward and throw my arms around his neck. "I'll do anything you say. You just bring her back to me, all right?"

I can feel his jowls bounce against my shoulder as he nods his head. "I can assure you that I will do everything within my power."

Time to pull myself together and launch Phase 1 of the attack. Hustling into the bathroom, I splash cold water on my face to reduce the sob-related eye puffiness, and scrape a comb through my hair.

A little mascara to detract from the redness and some lip tint will hopefully draw the eye away from the hot mess above.

I grab the bag of samples Doc Ledo collected for me and head toward the sliding bookcase door.

"Hold something back."

The clairaudient message drifts to me from the ether and I stop stark still.

Rummaging through the bag, I select one of the blood samples and one of the fiber samples and approach the hidden compartment. Below the bookcase, a large piece of raised paneling décor pops open when pressed firmly. I drop the two samples into the drawer and close it.

My eyes move to the rolling corkboard that normally contains all the 3 x 5 cards from the current investigation, and another wave of grief hits me. There's no need for a murder wall. I know exactly who stole my grandmother, and I'm going to get her back alive and well. And by *alive* I mean in her ghost form, and by *well* I mean exactly as she was before.

The chilly breeze gusting up from the great lake is a welcome touch on my hot, puffy face. I slow my pace and take several deep breaths as I stroll toward the sheriff's station.

The front desk is unmanned, and I'm grateful I don't have to speak to Furious Monkeys or creepy Deputy Candy. I hurry through the bullpen and make a sharp left turn into Erick's office.

Where I slam directly into the exiting Deputy Candy.

He scoops his unwelcome arms around me. "Well, hello there. Let me help you out, Miss Moon. Are you okay? What's in the bag?"

Yanking my arm away from him, I step back. "I'm fine. And I think you were just leaving."

He raises his eyebrows and regards me as though I'm the one who's crossed a line before walking out of Erick's office.

I close the door behind him.

"Geez, Moon. He was only trying to keep you from falling over."

"Look, I don't have time to debate the underlying motives of dodgy Deputy Candy. My grandmother has been kidnapped and Pyewacket was attacked."

Erick's first instinct is to grab his notepad and pen, but as my words roll around in his mind, a look of confusion twists his expression. "Hold on. You said your grandmother? You mean Isadora, the one who is a ghost?"

I collapse onto a sturdy but uncomfortable chair and sigh. "I know. Silas already told me there's no Penal Code for ghost-napping. But that crazy gypsy woman broke into my bookshop, injured Pyewacket, and literally stole my grandmother!"

Erick rubs a hand across his brow and scrapes back a loose chunk of sexy blond bangs. "Start from the beginning and try to remember you're talking to a guy who barely believes ghosts are real."

My eyes widen, and I gasp.

He waves his hands in surrender. "Wait, I believe you. I'm just saying it's a lot for me to take in. So explain it to me like I'm a kid. A kid who doesn't believe in ghosts."

Exhaling loudly, I blink back the tears already threatening to spill from my eyes and tell the tale as slowly as I can. However, I continue to indict the wicked gypsy and insist on retribution.

Erick leans back in his chair and nods slowly. "So the evidence you're talking about is in that bag?" He gestures to the small paper sack on my lap.

"Oh, right." I dump the contents of the bag onto his desk, and he examines the individually packaged specimens. "Doc Ledo did a great job collecting this evidence. We certainly have enough here to press charges on the breaking and entering and possibly animal cruelty. But you know there's nothing I can do about the ghost stuff."

"Yeah, I guess." My heart cracks a little more and a traitorous tear leaks from the corner of my eye.

Erick is up in a flash and at my side. "If it was up to boyfriend me, I'd toss her in a cell and throw away the key. But I uphold the law, and that law applies equally to all citizens. I think you better sleep on this. The evidence you brought me definitely places her at your bookshop—if that's her blood and her clothing. But she just agreed to drop similar charges against you. And I hate to be the one to tell you this next part, but the blood evidence collected from Pyewacket's paws is a double-edged sword."

I lay my head on his shoulder, snuffle, and suck

in a quick breath. "What do you mean, double-edged sword?"

"It would be very easy for her to say that a vicious wildcat attacked her. She could force you to put Pyewacket to sleep."

I bolt upright and look down at him in shock. "She wouldn't dare."

Erick gets to his feet and pulls me close. "Like I said, it's a double-edged sword. After what she did today, I don't think it's a good idea to make guesses about what she may or may not do next. Sleep on it. Talk to Silas. I know how your little supercomputer brain works. You'll come up with a viable plan by tomorrow."

I want to argue. I want to beat my fists against his chest like every romantic drama I have ever watched on the silver screen, but he's right. My eagerness to punish the gypsy could backfire. I have to weigh my options carefully and also admit I'm too emotional to make this massive decision today.

He pulls me close, and I lay my head on his chest and trace my finger along the outline of his badge. His woodsy-citrus scent comforts me as I listen to the steady thrumming of his heart.

He kisses the top of my head. "I'm not sure what I can do to help, but we'll get your grandmother back. If it's within my power, I will get it done."

"Thank you. That's what I needed to hear."

He tucks his finger under my chin and lifts my mouth to meet his.

The power of this kiss is everything. He's on my side. He's got my back.

CHAPTER 15

THE SHORT WALK back to the bookstore feels hollow and pointless. There's nothing there. No interfering ghost waiting to scare the bejeezus out of me, and no entitled feline to boss me around. When I reach the ornate wooden door, I crouch and run my fingers over the carving of the wildcat that bears a striking resemblance to Pyewacket. "I'll make things right, Mr. Cuddlekins. I promise."

Wandering between the stacks, I drag my fingers across the spines of the volumes my grandmother left me. In her absence, it's painfully obvious to me that the bookshop and its contents hold very little value without Isadora.

A noise from the back room stands my hairs on end. I hunker down and creep along the aisle. "I have a gun, and I know how to use it."

The responding cackle sends a wave of relief down my spine. "I doubt either of those things is true, kid." Twiggy saunters out of the back room, stomping her biker boots along the floor. "I'm back."

"No kidding. A text would've been nice." My heartbeat slowly returns to normal.

"Oh, a text, eh? I called you four times and you couldn't be bothered, but a text would've been the ticket. Why the heck are you so jumpy? Where's the spoiled cat?"

My defenses crumble, and Twiggy is forced to endure a flood of my tears before I find the strength to tell her my sad story.

Her hands ball into fists, and she narrows her gaze. "What are we waitin' for? Let's march over to that gypsy's hovel and set her straight."

"Silas is concerned about the new powers she's displaying since her acquisition of *Loca Sine Lumine, Loca Sine Lege*."

Twiggy shakes her head and pretends to spit. "I can't believe she snuck into this place to steal that book during a wedding! The woman has no manners whatsoever."

"Agreed. Silas told me to take care of Pye and leave the gypsy to him."

She chuckles and nods her head. "Yeah, I wouldn't want to land on the wrong side of that guy."

A heavy sigh escapes. "I don't know what to do without Grams."

Twiggy tramps toward me and pats me roughly on the back. "Don't fret, kid. If death couldn't keep Isadora down, I doubt very much some two-bit gypsy will succeed."

Every fiber of my being desperately wants to believe Twiggy and share her optimism, but my psychic senses refuse to get on board. Everything trickling in from the great beyond is laden with doubt and dread.

"I'm going to head upstairs and do a little research before I have to pick up Pyewacket."

She nods and returns to the back room without another word.

When I walk into the apartment and catch sight of the murder wall/lost dog investigation, I lose it. Ripping all the cards from the tacks, I tear them and throw them to the ground. I kick the rolling corkboard to teach it a lesson, but only succeed in sending a sharp pain shooting from my big toe up my leg.

"Stupid. Stupid. Stupid. How could I have let this happen? I'm supposed to be some kind of psychic. Why didn't any of my super-special superpowers warn me that Grams was in danger?"

Maybe they did. Maybe my preoccupation with the missing dog and the 1950s ghost got my signals crossed or messages misinterpreted. The bottom line is that it's up to me to get her back.

I march into the closet and run my fingers over the sacred couture. "What would you want me to wear, Grams?"

Silence.

Picking up a pair of dangerously high Jimmy Choos, I hold them above my head like the baby Simba in *The Lion King*. "If you come back to me, I promise I'll wear any shoes that you want any day of the week!"

Nothing.

My arms drop to my sides, and the shoes tumble onto the thickly carpeted floor. An instant pang of guilt stabs my heart. "Sorry. Sorry. I'll put them back on the shelf right now." I retrieve the shoes and carefully arrange them in the footwear Hall of Fame.

There's no response from the ether, and no otherworldly tingling in my mood ring. Desperation takes my bargaining to a new level.

Yanking open one of the built-in drawers, I grab a sexy negligée and wave it in the air. "If you come back to me, I'll wear this for Erick!"

Nada. Bupkus.

The flush that tinges my cheeks is part embarrassment and part frustration. This is beneath me. I'm a doer, not a beggar. I'm not going to sit here and feel sorry for myself, and bargain with invisible forces. I'm going to *do* something.

As I shove the negligée back in the drawer, my hand bumps the cold steel of my handgun.

My throat tightens and my conscience hits me with a thousand warnings.

Slipping the gun out of the drawer, I turn it over in my hand and grimace. "I hope it doesn't come to this." I place the weapon back in the drawer and slowly push it closed.

I honestly hope it doesn't come to that, but if it does . . .

Time to end this pity party and get crackin' like the super-sleuth heiress that I am!

Without bothering to wait for permission, I push through the swinging gate at the sheriff's station and coldly ignore the overreaching welcome from Deputy Candy.

Stopping in the doorway to Erick's office, I lean against the doorjamb, kick out a hip, and attempt a seductive grin.

He looks up from the reports on his desk and his surprise rapidly shifts to anticipation. "You look like a lady with something on her mind."

So far, so good. "I have several things on my mind, Sheriff Harper, not the least of which is our overnight Valentine's Day getaway." I flash my eyebrows, in case there is any confusion about my meaning.

Erick's pupils dilate, and he strides toward me with a naked hunger percolating in his eyes. "Go on." He scoops me into his office and closes the door.

I'm struggling with my options. Should I kiss him first and then ask the favor, or ask the favor and offer the smooch as the reward?

"I recognize that look, Moon."

Oops. I hesitated too long and lost my advantage. "I need a small favor."

He loosens his hold and sighs. "I should have known your performance was too good to be true."

"Rude."

He shrugs. "What do you need?"

"I was wondering if you could bring Mrs. Nowak in for questioning?"

He sits on the edge of his desk and scrunches up his face in confusion. "What for? I recommended you not press charges, because of how it could endanger Pyewacket."

"Sure. I get that part, but she doesn't know that, right? Couldn't you just bring her in and, you know, shake her up a little?"

He laughs out loud. "Shake her up a little? The woman is in her late sixties! Not that I advocate police violence with suspects of any age, but I'm certainly not going to threaten a woman of her age in such ill health."

My psychic antennae perk up and take notice of this newsflash. "Ill health? What do you mean?"

"When she came in to file the complaint about the break-in, she did not look well. Her skin was sallow, the bones in her face were too visible, and even the subtlest movements seemed to cause her pain."

I might actually be able to use this little tidbit. "So, is that a no?"

He narrows his gaze and tilts his head. "It's a hard pass on harassing Mrs. Nowak."

"Fair enough. It was worth a shot." I turn to leave, but he catches my hand and pulls me tight.

"Now that the favor topic has been shelved, I'd like to revisit the discussion of our getaway."

Beads of sweat pop out along my hairline, and my knees go wobbly. "What about it?"

"Am I making a reservation for one room or two?"

Dear Lord, baby Jesus! This can't be happening. I need more time. I need a distraction. "Do I have to decide today?"

"Valentine's is less than three days from now. I'm sure the inn would like to finalize my reservation."

His phrasing seems to indicate he's already reserved two rooms, so the worst thing that could happen as a result of my delay tactics would be that I don't have to face this "blue pill or red pill" choice today. "I have too much on my mind. Once Grams is back safe and sound—"

He presses a finger to my lips. "No more excuses, Moon. One room or two?"

My chest constricts.

The door to his office bursts open, and Deputy Candy marches in.

Hallelujah! It's actually the first time I've been happy to see this guy. "I better get going, Erick. Talk to you later."

Sheriff Harper exhales with force and shakes his head. "Yes, you will."

I push past Candy and hustle out of the station.

Normally I'd stick around to eavesdrop, but I can't take that kind of risk today. Especially not in the middle of such a delicate negotiation with a lawman.

I'm going to start by saying this isn't the best idea I've ever had. But there's literally no one to stop me. I tug on a mousy-brown, shoulder-length wig and bobby pin it into place just like Ghost-ma taught me. Next, I wipe the tears that are streaming down my cheek and apply a little lip tint.

My usual skinny jeans, high tops, and a T-shirt that says "Challenge Accepted" below a traffic signal with the yellow light on, will work perfectly for this undercover mission.

Oh, did I mention the wad of cash in my pocket? That's right, I'm not above bribery, should it be necessary.

Driving toward the hospital, I'm plagued by second thoughts. I push through and convince myself that it's a good idea.

My colorful résumé will serve me well tonight. I've cleaned more than my share of office buildings and restaurants, and I know for a fact that employees are always calling in sick or sometimes not showing up at all, and not bothering to make any excuse.

Luck is on my side. Someone from the custodial staff comes out the rear entrance of the hospital and unloads several bags of waste from his cart into a large dumpster.

Casually walking toward the door, I drop my keys and fiddle around retrieving them while he turns his cart to head back inside.

He taps his ID card against the keypad and pulls open the door. I silently scoot up behind him as he pushes through and grab the handle just before the door closes.

A quick ten-count ensures that he'll be down the hall when I slip in.

And . . . I'm in. So far, my plan is flawless.

Hastily putting distance between me and the door, I look for an orderly or a candy striper. Bingo. Candy striper it is.

"Hey, can you help me?"

The young redhead turns, and I'm not sure which one of us is more shocked.

"Mitzy?"

"Tatum?" Leave it to me to find the one person in the hospital that knows me on sight, despite the wig—Tally's daughter.

"Of course I can help you, Mitzy. Sorry, it just threw me to see you in that wig and in this part of the hospital. It's normally employees only. What do you need?"

Decisions, decisions. I decide to roll the dice and hope she buys what I'm selling. "I'm kind of doing one of those *Undercover Boss* things. The Duncan-Moon Foundation is getting ready to make a donation to the hospital, but I wanted to do some first-hand investigating. My plan was to work a shift on the custodial staff and see how things really run. Would you mind taking me to the supervisor's office and going along with my story?"

She smiles and claps me on the shoulder. "My mom was right about you. You really are the best. Of course I'll help you. Follow me."

Great. I've bamboozled a perfectly innocent and generous young girl. Instead of the thrill of victory, I'm feeling the sickening swirl of compromised values. Too late to turn back now. Looks like I'll be making an actual donation to the hospital to do proper penance.

Tatum walks me into the Environmental Services office and introduces me to the manager. "Mr. Osborne, I found this poor girl wandering around the floor. She's—" Her eyes widen and she freezes.

Thrusting my hand forward, I jump in. "Darcy Brown. The temp agency sent me over to fill in for someone who called in sick. Just give me a cart and tell me which floor to start on."

The baffled Mr. Osborne stares at me and chews his lower lip. "Someone called in sick? What agency?" Before he can think of any additional questions, his phone rings. "Mr. Osborne here. I see. Well, I'm sorry to hear that. You take care." He gently places the receiver back in the cradle and looks up at me in awe. "That was my first-floor guy. He just called in sick."

I smile and nod. "Like I said, just give me a cart and tell me where to start."

My accidental rhyme hits a positive note with the confused Mr. Osborne, and he grabs a spare key card from his top right drawer. "Thank you, Tatum. I'll take it from here."

She smiles at me, winks unnecessarily, and departs.

"Follow me, Miss Brown."

Fortunately, I've used this fake identity enough times that I actually remember to respond. "You bet."

He leads me to a large storage room filled with janitorial carts, cleaning supplies, and racks of toilet paper and paper towel refills.

"You can grab that cart there, and here's your key." He hooks it through a metal ring on the side of the cart. "Your shift doesn't start for half an hour, but if you want to clock in early, that's fine by me. It'll give you a chance to get acquainted with the layout on the first floor."

He rattles off a list of departments and shares several special requests that I will certainly forget, but there is one thing he mentions that brings a warm inner glow to my heart: medical records is also on the first floor.

Medical records is the only reason I'm here. "Copy that, Mr. Osborne. Is there a night supervisor, or anyone I should check in with if I have a question?"

"Nah. Everyone mostly keeps to their floor, but if you get confused, or forget something, you can come in here and use one of those radios to reach the night security. They'll be roaming the floors, but I'll let them know you've been cleared for first floor."

"Great. Thanks very much."

He leaves, mumbling under his breath about my uncanny timing, and I stand in the janitorial closet bursting with anticipation.

One thing I learned from my extensive movie and television education is that if there is a radio, it must be tucked under a towel in one's cart. Later, when I help myself to a peek at the records, I'll need to keep tabs on those roving security guards.

CHAPTER 16

MY NATURAL DISLIKE of hospitals has lessened during my time in Pin Cherry. To be fair, this particular institution has saved the lives and mended the injuries of a number of my closest friends. I'm pleased that the first floor is rapidly emptying as the administrative offices close for the day and employees scurry from their cubicles.

A somewhat colorful history, on several cleaning crews, prepared me perfectly for this ruse. I'm emptying waste bins, cleaning windows, and dusting desks and countertops. Deep down, I'm hoping that the coast will clear for operation Sneak a Peek, long before I have to do any serious work.

One of the security officers makes a pass through the first floor and offers me a friendly head nod and a finger gun.

I smile and throw him a harmless coworker wink.

He struts off toward the elevator, and I slip into an empty supervisor's office to catch the radio traffic.

Crackling and static. "That new girl on the first floor is a hottie. You wanna take the next pass in an hour and check her out?"

Security guard number two quickly replies, "10-4. Maybe she's supply-closet worthy."

Gross. I cross my fingers in hopes that my mission is complete long before security guard number two comes a leering.

Turning down the volume and slipping the radio back into its hiding place, I reenter the main hallway and check for any stragglers.

Ladies and gentlemen, the coast is clear.

Trundling toward the records office, I swipe at a couple of countertops and clear three windowless rooms that could be concealing dedicated employees.

The records office beckons me like a shining beacon. The brown plastic sign with its thick, white sans serif letters draws me as a moth to the flame. I swipe my key card and pull my cart inside behind me. No point in leaving a calling card in the hallway, should security guard number two make an early pass.

My janitorial history includes libraries, restaurants, and office buildings. No hospitals. However, taking into consideration my television education, I know that records are not stored in alphabetical order. Patients are given numbers, and those numbers are stored—in a tech-less town like Pin Cherry—on microfilm.

The hospital's machine is not the same as the one at the Pin Cherry Library. Rather than spools, here we have 4 x 6 sheets of film that lie on a glass plate and are moved around under the reader which projects the image onto a screen.

It takes some finagling to figure out the correct direction to move the piece of film in order to see what I want, but after a couple minute's practice with a random sheet, I'm a pro. I search through the card-catalog style drawers and locate the piece of film containing names starting with the letters "N-o-w."

Laying the film on the plate, I slide it into position and grab the six-digit code for Ania Karina Nowak's medical records.

A moment of temptation bubbles up as I spy the drawer marked "Ha - Ho."

Nope. Bending the law is one thing, secretly perusing my boyfriend's medical records is quite another. I'm not gonna cross that line.

However . . .

My hands move to the "Do - Du" drawer and I quickly locate the code for Isadora Duncan. There's no harm in checking a dead woman's records.

My breath catches in my throat. *I miss you, Grams.*

Carefully replacing every item in the exact place I found it, I move to the physical files. They are six shelves high, with the top shelf above my head, and I hope I don't need a stepstool. The last thing I want is to fall in the records room, knock myself unconscious, and get busted by security.

Hooray! Mrs. Nowak's name falls in a section of the shelf just below eye level. I pull out the file and search for recent entries.

Bingo. She's suffering from severe aortic stenosis and peripheral arterial disease.

The moment I identify her illness and read the doctor's projection of her remaining months to live, my moody mood ring flares to life.

The image reveals a powerful Silas Willoughby transmuting time and space as he dishes out retribution.

She wants Silas angry and vengeful. Why? The words flow through the ether like a dangerous whisper. "To die."

What? She wants to die? I snap a picture of the pertinent information on my phone, replace the file, and search for my grandmother's folder.

Holy moly! Isadora's file is over an inch thick. No time to view that now. I wedge the hefty manila folder under my shirt and tuck it into the back of my waistband. Once I replace my coat, the bulge is barely noticeable.

Time to hightail it out of the records room, and the hospital.

Barely thirty seconds elapse before the elevator pings and security guard number two, I'm assuming, struts onto the floor.

He strides toward me purposefully. His swagger sends a wave of nausea through my gut.

"What's cookin' good lookin'?"

He can't be serious. Time for Mitzy Moon to make a grand exit and end this charade.

He winks and licks his lips.

Going where the material leads me, I hunch over and grab my stomach. "Oh no! Morning sickness!" Using all of my acting skills to fake gag, I struggle to hold back imaginary regurgitation as I run toward the back door.

"Hold on, gorgeous. I can hold your hair back for ya."

Get a load of this guy! I might actually spew.

Busting out the back door, I pull my coat tight to keep the file from escaping and hustle to the Jeep. Hopping inside, I floor it and fishtail out of the parking lot. The great thing about winter is that ice really lends itself to dramatic getaways.

It's probably too late to call Silas, even with information this juicy. Plus, I want to rifle through Isadora's file guilt-free. Once I admit what I've done, he's sure to arrive on my doorstep with a heaping helping of condemnation.

The site of the animal hospital on my right hits me like a slap across the face. Shoot! Pyewacket! How could I forget my poor little fur baby? I turn into the parking lot and check my phone. It's after 8:00 p.m.

Running to the doors, I'm unsurprised to find them locked. Standing in front of the entrance, I weigh my options. I could call the emergency number to see if—

My phone dings with a text notification.

"hi frgt 2 text. i got pye"

Wow. Stepbrothers can come in real handy. Especially ones with after-school jobs at veterinary clinics. I definitely caught a lucky break on that one. Pyewacket would never have forgiven me for leaving him at the clinic overnight.

The glowing marquee of our local Italian restaurant catches my eye, and I turn in to grab some takeout lasagna for dinner.

Whether it's an extrasensory thing or big sister thing, I can't be sure, but a wonderful idea pops to mind. "Do you have a reservation for Stellen Jablonski on Valentine's Day?"

The owner's son runs his finger down the list of names in the book and smiles. "I do. Reservation for two at 7:00 p.m. on the fourteenth. Did you need to make a change?"

"No, not at all. I was wondering if I could pre-pay for his dinner?"

He looks up and smiles. "Of course. That's so generous. How much did you want to put on account?"

"No idea. What's a good amount? Dinner for two, appetizers, desserts . . ."

"Did you want to include a tip?"

"Absolutely. Would a hundred be enough?"

His eyes widen. "More than enough."

My to-go order comes out, and we complete our transactions.

There. I have a few surprises of my own, Stellen.

After suffering the slings and arrows of an un-grateful wildcat, I abandon Pyewacket to his im-promptu sleepover at the penthouse. Stellen created a small feline infirmary in my dad's living room, complete with a saucer of cream, a bowl of Fruity Puffs, and pizza cut into cat-sized bites.

I mean, I'm sure Pye is uneasy about returning to the scene of the attack at the bookshop, but clearly his refusal to accompany me back to the apartment was caused by more than trepidation.

The loudest sound in the Bell, Book & Candle is the beat of my heart as I make my way upstairs with the aid of the light on my phone.

First things first. I change into my reindeer onesie pajamas and drag a space heater over to the settee. It doesn't take long to polish off the lasagna, which leads me to the stolen files.

I'm sure Silas will warn me about the legal ramifications of stealing medical records, but Isadora Duncan has passed away, and, if I can't bask in the glory of her designer ghost, at least I can learn something about her past in these documents.

The recent entries all pertain to the terminal illness that took her life months before I arrived in town. As she's always indicated, the doctors blamed a history of alcoholism as the catalyst for her multiple organ failures.

As I delve deeper into the reports from years before, it's evident there were several asymptomatic incidents, seemingly unrelated to her cause of death, which landed her in the hospital. Reading between the lines, and leaning into my extrasensory perceptions, I can see where her hunger for magical knowledge and tendency to drive her explorations beyond the limits of her physical body could easily have led to her untimely demise.

Regardless of the parade of last names that dance through the paperwork, the Duncan surname seems to have served as the constant in her file.

The waxing moon peeking through the large 6 x 6 windows that face the great lake draws my gaze from the page, and a quick check of my phone confirms it's time to turn in.

My curiosity delays me a moment longer, and I flip to the oldest entries in the file.

The hairs on the back of my neck tingle the moment my eyes discover the word "miscarriage."

I run my fingers down the sheet, check the dates, and note the name at the top of the sheet. Myrtle Isadora Johnson.

My hands go weak and the file drops into my lap.

Odell and Grams had a child. Perhaps it was the loss of her baby rather than the feud between Odell and Cal that pushed her so deep into the bottle.

Closing the file, I lay it tenderly on the coffee table and stumble to bed.

As I lie in the large, four-poster slice of heaven, I stare at the ceiling and flick through the images and ideas bouncing around my consciousness.

Odell never remarried. Maybe the loss of my grandmother isn't the only hurt he's nursing.

No wonder Isadora doted so extravagantly on my father. I don't have any kids, and I'm not sure I ever will, but it doesn't take an empath to imagine the depth of pain and suffering that losing one's child would cause.

A wave of guilt rushes over me, and my eyelids refuse to close. I never expected to find something like this. I guess that's why it's not a good idea to stick your nose where it doesn't belong. I'm sure Silas will have a long prepared speech to dump all over me once he finds out what I've done.

All I can do now is pray that we find a way to get Isadora's ghost back, and that I have a chance to confess my sin directly to her.

The emotional exhaustion of the last couple of days finally drags me under. My dreams are filled with hope, and my nightmares are fraught with deadly confrontations with the gypsy and sinister images of the grim reaper, plague doctors, and, for some reason, the flaming eye of Sauron.

Morning finds me exhausted and highly agitated. Time to pull my mentor into my web and hope that he'll find it in his heart to forgive my transgressions.

CHAPTER 17

THE COFFEE IS BREWING, and my eyes are barely open. There's a distinctive scratching on the metal door leading to the alleyway.

Opening the door, I glance down at my fiendish feline. "Welcome home, traitor."

Pyewacket saunters past me and allows his tail to thwack me on the leg. He proceeds directly to the cabinet holding his favorite sugary children's cereal and plops expectantly onto his haunches.

"Oh, I see how this works. You run off and spend the night wherever you want and the second you come home, I'm supposed to drop everything."

"Reow." Can confirm.

I crouch and scratch him roughly between his black-tufted ears. "You have to stop scaring the living daylights out of me, Pye. I know you were trying to protect Grams, and I do appreciate that. But I'd be lost without you. Do you understand?"

He places his front paw on my knee, rises up and licks my cheek.

The gesture brings tears to my eyes. "What's your deal, son? You're so flippin' smart!"

"RE-OW!" Game on!

"I know, right? We're gonna get Grams back and teach this gypsy a lesson she'll never forget."

His only response is a casual shoulder nudge to the cabinet holding his Fruity Puffs.

I pour him a large bowl, gulp down a few swigs of java, and call my alchemist.

Once I spill the beans about my undercover operation, the voice emanating from my speakerphone pulls no punches.

"Mizithra Achelois Moon! Not only was that a dangerous plan, but highly illegal. Medical records are protected by a number of state and federal laws, and breaking into a hospital records office is certain to carry punishments that even I could not erase."

I'm pleased he can't see the smirk on my face. "I wore a disguise. The only person that even knew I was there is Tatum. And she thinks I was doing some undercover work for the foundation."

Silas harrumphs. "So where will I be making the donation?"

"How about something to pediatrics? That's always good for PR, right?"

Shockingly, my comment brings a chuckle. "Why don't I pick up some pastries and two large coffees at Bless Choux and join you at the bookshop presently?"

"That would be divine." Where did that come from? Must be the weight of the guilt wreaking havoc on my vocab. "By the way, Pyewacket is home safe, and I don't think that mishap should count as one of his lives. Do you?"

A true belly laugh echoes from my mobile before Silas manages an answer. "I agree. I believe the count remains at five. Is that correct, Robin Pyewacket Goodfellow?"

"Reow." Can confirm.

By the time Silas arrives with the blessed sustenance, I've changed out of my pajamas and even managed to brush my hair like a big girl.

The chocolate croissant never ceases to tantalize my pallet, and the subtle hazelnut undertone in the secret Bless Choux coffee blend offers a magical combination.

Silas moves the pink pastry box, catches sight of the thick medical file on the coffee table, and stares at me in horror. "You stole the entire file? I thought you simply took a picture of the pertinent information."

Uh oh. Looks like it's time for true confessions, round two. "That's not Mrs. Nowak's file."

Silas reclines into the scalloped-back and interlaces his fingers expectantly.

After a difficult swallow and a deep breath to steady myself, I come clean. "That's Isadora's file."

"Mizithra!"

"I know. I know. It was wrong, but I miss her so much. I thought maybe I could learn something that would help us get her back." I stare at him pleadingly and rub the back of my hand.

Silas eyes me suspiciously. "Your body language is at odds with your words, my dear."

I flop onto the settee, and all the air rushes out of my lungs. "All right. I was curious. She's dead and gone, and her ghost is rather tightlipped. Did you know that—?"

Silas raises his hand, and I'm not sure whether it's the gesture or an alchemical transmutation that freezes the words on my tongue. "It is not your place to share your grandmother's secrets. I cannot undo what you have done. However, when Isadora is returned to us, I shall expect a full confession of your deeds. I will leave your punishment to her, as it is her protected world that you have invaded."

Well, now I feel like a giant pile of— "Understood. That's more than fair." Leaning forward, I attempt to redeem a small portion of my compromised morals. "I resisted the urge to look at Erick's file. I didn't even pull the microfilm to get the digits." My smile is a tad triumphant, but my timid gaze longs for understanding.

"I should think not! The very idea." He nods vigorously, and his jowls bounce beneath his red cheeks. "Indeed. Now, what is this information you obtained, so unethically, regarding Mrs. Nowak?"

"She's dying." I share the diagnosis and the prognosis and wait for his reply.

"And you're sure the message you heard was 'to die'?"

"Yeah, I'm sure. Why?"

"If you connect all the data points, I'm not sure your conclusion is the only one we may reach."

"Silas, you're talking in riddles. If you don't think she's trying to incite you to end her life before the ravages of the disease take her, what other conclusion is there?"

He leans back, steeples his fingers, and bounces his chin on the tip of his pointer.

Oh boy! Here comes a lesson.

"Close your eyes and review the events that have occurred since the young girl's dog went missing."

"You think Yolo is connected to the gypsy?"

"Close your eyes and review."

I do as I'm told. Letting my eyelids fall, I take

several deep, cleansing breaths, try not to chuckle or think of Sedona gurus, and let my mind pull up the images.

Yolo—a vision in purple.

The dog—friendly, obedient, innocent.

The tunnel—mysterious, otherworldly.

The repair—a gesture of love.

The tinker—harmless, clueless, eager to make a buck.

The disappearance—shocking, inexplicable, terrifying.

The camera— My eyes pop open. "Maybe she was planning on using the camera on herself! Maybe she wants to cross over and we ruined her plan!"

Silas nods and smooths his mustache with his thumb and forefinger. "As you can see, there are subtleties. Her kidnapping of your grandmother's ghost may not be malicious. Perhaps she intends to use Isadora as a bargaining chip."

The color drains from my face, and a sickening swirl grips my stomach. "But we destroyed the camera. We don't have anything to bargain with."

Silas nods solemnly and stares out the windows. "Perhaps, perhaps not."

"What do you mean?" My heart thumps in my chest, and the chill of knowing grips me.

He takes a moment to savor a sip of coffee.

"Mrs. Nowak has been seeking arcane knowledge for some time. She delves too quickly and with little regard for her personal health. At some juncture she must have realized the cost of her relentless pursuit. Based on her prognosis, her condition is beyond the point of reversal."

"That's why she wants to die?" The idea fights with the otherworldly messages wrestling for my attention.

"She correctly ascertained the existence of Isadora's ghost. You may be correct in assuming that she intended to experiment with the camera. However, the gypsy is a devout Catholic—"

"But she's a witch!"

"The two may coexist. Magic, philosophy, religion, alchemy—there is a cord that binds them all."

My shoulders slump under the weight of this idea. "But isn't suicide a mortal sin in Catholicism?"

He sighs and brushes pastry crumbs from his bushy mustache. "Indeed. I believe you must request a parley with the gypsy. We may have nothing to offer, at least nothing discernible. However, it will behoove us to gather additional information if we are to have any chance of recovering Isadora."

Collecting my phone from the sofa, I pace across the thick Persian rug as I place the call to Mrs. Nowak. It's safe to say my penance has officially begun. Tapping the speakerphone on gives me the advantage of any ideas that may occur to my mentor.

"Hallo, Ania's Emporium."

"Good morning, Mrs. Nowak, it's Mitzy Moon."

A brief silence hangs between us. "I've been expecting your call, little thief." Her thick Polish accent hides none of her gloating.

Silas shakes his head in a clear warning against snarky retorts and frowns.

So much for returning her insult with one of my own. Apparently, I have to take the high road and put the "more flies with honey" theory to the test. "I never should have broken into your shop, and I'm genuinely sorry about that. Would you agree to meet with me?"

"Why? Why this meeting?" Her breathing is labored.

"I need my grandmother back. I must have something I can offer you in exchange."

Soft muttering and a cross between a scoff and possibly a spit is my only reply.

"Mrs. Nowak, I know why you wanted the camera. I'm willing to help you if I can."

A gasp followed by a tiny squeak, and then she must've dropped the phone. Glancing toward Silas, I lift a hand and shrug.

He gestures for me to simmer down and wait.

"Come to my shop. One hour. Bring the wizard."

Before I can correct her error, Silas nods and waves it away with a flick of his wrist.

"I'll be there—we'll be there, Mrs. Nowak. Thank you."

"Pshaw." The line goes dead.

Looking from the blank screen of my phone to my mentor, I scrunch up my face and ask, "Do you think it's a trap?"

Silas works his mouth back and forth as he seems to literally chew on my question. "It may be a trap, or you may have something that she wants. The question you must ask yourself before we proceed is: Will you be willing to meet her demand?"

Dropping my phone on the coffee table, I wring my hands and choke back a sob. "I would do anything to get Grams back."

Silas slowly rises from the chair and strides toward me. "Would you give Mrs. Nowak your mood ring?"

I clutch my left hand to my chest and cover it with my right. "Why my mood ring? She doesn't even know what it does, does she?"

Silas harrumphs. "Before you enter into a negotiation, you must be clear about what you are willing to lose. You are not willing to do *anything* to facilitate Isadora's return. Perhaps you can spend the next forty-five minutes weighing your options. Decide what it is you are truly willing to risk and see that you bend the negotiation in the direction you wish to take. If you enter into this parley without a goal or an exit strategy, you will either fail miserably or sacrifice far more than you can afford. And I'm sure you realize I'm not speaking in terms of finances."

Struggling to swallow, I loosen my hold on the mood ring and glance around the apartment. Maybe I'm not willing to do anything? "I see your point. I'll think things over and try to come up with a strategy. But what if she wants something from you?"

Silas exhales and clasps my shoulder firmly. "I have erected a clear set of boundaries in my life, Mitzy. I know myself, and I am all too familiar with my limits. I shall support you to the very edge of them, but not beyond."

"Copy that."

He slips out of the apartment and busies himself in the Rare Books Loft.

I step into the closet and drop onto the padded mahogany bench. For some reason, this is where I feel closest to her. This is where I can best "weigh my options" and come up with a workable strategy for the negotiations.

As I ponder my next move, a blur of tan races into the closet and leaps onto the bench.

Scratching the softer fur under his chin, I share my dilemma. "I have to decide what I'm willing to sacrifice, Pye. It's a lot harder than I imagined. I thought I would give up anything to get her back, but that's not true."

"Ree-oow." Conspiratorial agreement.

My eyes travel over the nearly endless content of my walk-in wardrobe. The elegant blue dress I wore to Kitty Zimmerman-Duncan's ladies lunch, the adorable black dress with its red cherries that Grams insisted I wear to the Pin Cherry Festival, the sexy black boots that put my undercover disguise over the top as an anthropology student at Birch County Community College . . . Isadora was always there for me. Always supporting my crazy plans and helping me pull myself together to complete the missions required to solve cases and help people. What will I do without her?

Pye rubs his head against my shoulder, as though he's reading my mind.

I suppose the real question is, what will I do to get her back?

CHAPTER 18

SILAS APPEARS in the doorway with a look that combines empathy and warning. "It is time."

Time is up. We have to go and meet the gypsy and hope we can find a way to save my grand-mother. To be honest, I don't think I used my time very wisely. I mostly reminisced, and, when I wasn't doing that, I was feeling sorry for myself. I didn't really come up with any boundaries. I probably confused myself more than I already was.

Rising from the bench, I stroke Pyewacket's head and smile down at him. "You watch the shop while we're gone, all right?"

"Reow." Can confirm.

"But don't risk your life! If things get dicey, run."

He blinks his eyes slowly. It's a tolerant gesture that I've come to interpret as subtle disagreement.

Silas seems to have taken the same interpretation, and his soft chuckle lightens the mood. "Come, Mizithra. One mustn't be late to such an important engagement."

We load into my vehicle, and I drive at a surprisingly reasonable speed. This does not escape the notice of my mentor.

"It would appear that you are in no great hurry to face Mrs. Nowak."

"You're not wrong. I definitely want Grams back, and the sooner the better, but I didn't really come to any shattering decisions during my interminable forty-five-minute wait."

He harrumphs and adjusts his seatbelt. "I should like to do most of the talking, in light of your undefined boundaries. To be clear, the goal of this negotiation is to understand what the gypsy will accept in exchange for the safe return of Isadora."

Taking my eyes off the road for a moment, I flash Silas a look of disdain. "What are you saying? I thought we were going there to get Grams back?"

"Then you would be sadly mistaken. This is the first step of the process. If Mrs. Nowak required something as simple as the coat off your back or a yet to be determined sum of money, she would not have escalated things to this height. The knowledge and energy required to kidnap your grandmother's ghost is substantial. A woman looking for an easy payout would not have gone to such lengths. You must prepare yourself for the magnitude of what may be required. I shall, of course, protect you from overstepping, but that is not to say the pound of flesh will be taken painlessly."

A heaviness settles over me, and I feel the subtle pressure of suffocation on my chest and throat. I'm not ready. My film-based education and my cursory knowledge of alchemy have not prepared me for such a dangerous game. Silas calmly places his hand on the steering wheel, and, as my focus returns to the road in front of me, I can see why. "Holy space cadet! I totally forgot I was driving."

"Indeed."

How the man can remain so calm and unruffled, I will never know. If I could mimic a fraction of that steadiness, I may be able to make it through this confrontation without promising her my firstborn child, or possibly my soul. The emporium looms into view, and a sickening chill flutters through my body when I turn off the engine.

Silas takes my hand and mumbles something almost under his breath.

As I open my mouth to ask what he said, a calming warmth flows up my arm, across my shoulders, to the top of my head, and then cascades all the way down to my toes.

"Thank you."

He smiles and pats my hand. "Follow me."

We approach the front door, and he politely holds it open for me. Once inside, the now-familiar mixture of herbs, incense, and scented soaps fills my nostrils. My throat tightens and I cough to clear the airway. "Mrs. Nowak? Mrs. Nowak, are you here?"

The response that greets me nearly knocks me off my feet.

"Mitzy! Mitzy! I knew you'd come for me!"

My body curls in on itself as though I've been shot, and my eyes fill with unshed tears.

Silas grips my arm and gazes at me questioningly.

Ghost-ma sweetens the deal. "She can't hear me! Trust me, I've called her every name in the book and she's done nothing. Our secret is safe!"

The corner of my mouth turns up, and I lean on Silas for support. "Grams is all right. She's talking to me."

His thick eyebrows arch, and he nods. "How useful."

Hoping against hope that, despite her kidnapping, she's retained her powers, I press my lips together and fire off a thought message. *I miss you so much! We're absolutely going to get you out of here!*

"I never doubted you for a minute, sweetie."

Mrs. Nowak clatters through the bead curtain, and I whisper a hasty secret to Silas. "Grams can still hear my thoughts."

He smiles and nods as though I've simply told him the time.

"No tricks." The gypsy dangles a beautiful glowing amulet in one hand and brandishes a large steel hammer in the other.

I gasp in horror as my brain struggles to comprehend the unspoken threat.

Silas steps forward and raises both of his hands in a gesture of surrender. "We have not come to hoodwink you, Mrs. Nowak. We come in peace and hope for an amicable resolution. Please, begin."

She lays the amber pendant on a stocky wooden table displaying decks of tarot cards, and I hold my breath while I wait to see what she has planned for the hammer. Thankfully, she places it next to the pendant and claps her hands twice.

As I wait for a Clapper-activated light to switch on, Silas stiffens. "What? What did she do?"

The gypsy grins, and the gold-cap over her eyetooth glistens. "The trap is set."

I don't know about you, but I'm still a little hung up on the gold tooth. That's definitely new.

Silas asks the question I should have. "Why did you call this meeting?"

I wish I could say that I hear the gypsy's reply, but Grams is blurting out information faster than I can process it.

"She has a death wish! Or maybe I should say a ghost wish. The nerve of this woman. She thought she could manipulate Silas by holding me for ransom. Don't listen to her, Mitzy. She's as phony as a two-dollar bill!"

I think you mean a three-dollar bill, Grams. We actually have two-dollar bills. Not that you'd waste your time with anything less than a Benjamin.

"Oh Mitzy! You're such a hoot!"

A movement beside me interrupts my spirit chat. Silas strides forward, and his spine straightens as he rises into his full power. "Ania, your mother would not want her precious grimoire abused in this way. We know that your time on this plane is coming to an end. Stealing *Loca Sine Lumine, Loca Sine Lege,* and trapping Isadora in that pendant, cannot change your fate. Give us what we came for and we shall never bother you again."

She takes a step forward and energy crackles around her like the snaps of static electricity on a blanket in the darkness. "You take nothing. I give nothing. I want to be like her." Her finger points dramatically at the amulet encasing my grandmother's ghost.

I can't comprehend why she wants this. "You

want to be a ghost? Why would you want to be a ghost? If you only have a few months to live, don't you want to be with your family? Don't your children want to see you one more time?"

My psychic senses pick up on a tidal wave of sorrow that nearly consumes Mrs. Nowak.

"Ania, what's wrong? Where are your children?"

Her rheumy eyes are rimmed by red lids, which fail to contain her tears. "They leave me. I am embarrassment. Evil witch. They couldn't escape fast enough."

Walking closer, in spite of my dislike for this woman, my heart hurts with her pain. "I know what it's like to live without family. I lost my mother when I was eleven. I thought I'd be alone for the rest of my life. Opening your heart is a risk, but every time I've taken that risk since I came to Pin Cherry, my life has been richer for it. I found my father, I have a stepmom, and a stepbrother." I have to pause and draw an emotion-laden breath. "My grandmother is the most important thing in the world to me. If I help you—" My tears are flowing unabated now. "If I help you mend fences with your children, will you please give me back my grandmother?"

Her thin shell of hatred cracks, and the pain of

loss seeps from the fractures like yolk from a broken egg.

"Ania, you and I have no quarrel. Whatever stood between you and my grandmother died with her. Let me help you make things right with your children."

Regret and relief wash over her wrinkled visage, but she stands her ground. "I don't want pain. The pain is too much." She rubs her right hand along her left arm and winces.

In addition to the pain of her terminal illness, I'd be willing to bet that arm bears the marks of the indefatigable Pyewacket.

Silas moves closer to her and offers her a small blue vial. "Place two grains in a cup of elderflower tea each morning. The pain will subside and you may focus on healing your family, before it's too late."

Her natural suspiciousness flares up, and she pulls her hand back for a moment. "No tricks?"

Silas wags his jowls. "Absolutely none."

She snatches the vial from his hand and slips it into her cleavage. "If this works"—she pats her bosom—"tomorrow this one helps me with the children. Then I return the ghost." She gestures to the amulet on the table.

Every fiber of my being wants to scream, "No!" I want to lunge toward the table and take whatever punishment her trap has to offer, so long as I get my hands on that amber pendant.

"Don't do anything stupid, sweetie. I heard her reading the spells out loud. I think there's a very good chance that you could lose your entire hand."

Right! Grams can hear everything I'm thinking. *Copy that. I'll keep my hands to myself.*

"Good girl."

Silas bows slightly and nods his head. "We have an accord, Mrs. Nowak. Mitzy will return tomorrow morning to assist in contacting your family. We appreciate this opportunity to start anew."

Her sadness and vulnerability vanish in the blink of an eye. She steps behind the table and retrieves the hammer. "You go now."

Without another word, Silas grips my elbow and steers me, quite against my will, out of the emporium.

A heavy silence consumes the drive back to the bookshop. It fills every corner of the vehicle and seems to make speech impossible.

My swanky apartment feels like a cheap hotel. The façade of elegance is meaningless without its creator.

"Why did you let her keep Grams?"

Silas drops into the scalloped-back chair and exhales as he rests his hands on his round belly. "Your grandmother is in no immediate danger—"

"How can you say that? That crazy gypsy was waving a hammer around over the amulet!"

"I should think your gifts would have shown you the lack of intent in her actions. What we saw was playacting, posturing. Would you not agree?"

There is nothing to prevent me from rolling my eyes and scoffing. "What I would say is that she is suffering physically and emotionally. My special *gifts* lead me to believe the ache in her heart is more uncomfortable than the pain in her body."

"Agreed. We shall reclaim Isadora in due time. I suggest you spend the remainder of the day gathering what information you can of Mrs. Nowak's descendants. If her claim that they abandoned her due to an aversion to the dark arts is true, that is a simple fix. If, however, there are deeper wounds at play, you must be prepared. Your success is all that stands between us and your grandmother."

"Great. No pressure, Silas."

He chuckles and flicks his wrist halfheartedly, as though my success is a foregone conclusion.

"Hey, what about the book? You didn't say anything about getting the book back as part of our negotiation."

He smooths his mustache and nods. "She will return the book. Focus your energies on the family matters and the rest will follow."

Sadly, the phrase *Family Matters* immediately

brings Urkel to mind, and I can't keep the voice in my head from asking, "Did I do that?"

Silas tilts his head. "Did I say something to amuse you?"

Shaking my head, I smile. "Trust me, it's not worth explaining. I'm going to head over to City Hall and see what I can find in the birth records. Unless you happen to know the names of her children?" I raise my eyebrows hopefully.

"I do not. I have some research to complete, and then I must return home to check on my experiments. Give Pyewacket my best when you see him."

"I think you mean 'if' I see him. He's been spending a lot of time with Stellen."

My mentor nods as though my complaint makes perfect sense. "The boy suffered a great loss with the recent death of his father. Pye is simply offering him comfort."

Crossing my arms over my chest like a spoiled child, I mumble, "I could use some comfort, too."

A mischievous twinkle lights the alchemist's eyes. "You could always confide in Sheriff Harper."

My jaw drops. My cheeks redden, and I scoot out of the apartment without another word.

CHAPTER 19

THE OUTSIDE TEMPERATURE is slowly pushing the mercury up, but it's still not warm enough to walk to City Hall.

My previous trips to the clerk's office have trained me to be patient, vague, and never ask for copies of anything. That way lies madness. More forms, fees, and waiting periods. All I need is a believable story, and a moment or two of privacy for snapping pics with my phone.

There's a plethora of parking in the central square of the historic district, which, if you ask me, describes the entire town.

Since Pin Cherry Harbor is also the county seat of Birch County, our city hall contains county records too. The impressive structure is picture perfect, reminding me of the courthouse from *To Kill*

A Mockingbird. Three stories of solid granite with copper parapet walls, beautiful terrazzo floors, ornamental plaster cornices, and marble walls in the elevator lobby. Everyone considers it the height of architectural design in the region.

The clerk looks as old as the building and takes a millennium to close her magazine and creep toward me at a sloth's pace.

"Good afternoon, ma'am. I'm working on a genealogy project for submission to the historical society, and I need to examine some birth certificates. Would you be able to help me with that?"

She slips her bifocals from the top of her head to her nose and pushes a notepad across the well-worn wooden counter. "Write the names here, and if they were born in Birch County, I'll find them. Did you want to pick up copies next week?"

Much like a Boy Scout, I'm prepared. "Oh no, I don't need copies. I'm trying to get this project in before the deadline, so I'll just wait while you pull what you have and then I'll make some notes."

"How many records did you need?" Her eyes blink rapidly behind the glasses, and I feel her concern deepen.

"I'm not sure. I only have the mother's name, and I was hoping you could search by that."

Her demeanor shifts, and I sense a kernel of suspicion looking to sprout.

Better head that off at the pass. "I'm sure it couldn't be more than two or three. I know with your expertise that should be no problem."

Unbelievable. Flattery does the trick. "Well, I do have a knack for remembering things."

"I thought so." Gratuitous wink. "Here's the name." I write Ania Karina Nowak on the notepad and push it across the countertop to the clerk.

She gazes at the name and recognition flashes across her face. At first, I assume it's simply because she's worked in City Hall for so long, and has a vague familiarity with likely every resident of Pin Cherry, but my extrasensory perception picks up another thread. She's dealt with this woman. Perhaps even purchased something from this woman. I'd love to pull that thread and unravel the secrets of the seemingly straight-laced County Clerk, but I have a far more pressing quest.

She clears her throat and rips the top sheet off the notepad. "Have a seat in the waiting chairs, dear. This will take a few minutes."

I'm dying to run down the street and grab a pastry and hot coffee, but I don't want to give her any excuse to interrupt her search. Sitting in the chair, I stare at the rack of forms and the plain, uninviting atmosphere.

Erick! I can't explain the connection, other than

maybe this drab wasteland makes me long for something far more inviting.

As I begin tapping out a text, but before I press send, my conscience assures me this is something I should handle face-to-face, or, at the very least, voice-to-voice. I dial the sheriff's station and ask to be put through. "Hey, I have some bad news." Classic me. Tact? Who needs it? I can picture him in a track stance with one hand on his gun as he asks if I need to be rescued.

"Sorry for the abrupt start. But you know how fond I am of getting to the point. I'm not in any danger. Buuuut, things have gotten rather complicated with the gypsy and getting my grandmother back. I don't think I'm going to be available for a Valentine's getaway."

The silence on the other end of the phone nearly breaks my heart. I wish I could explain the life-threatening details of why I can't leave town in the middle of such a delicate negotiation, but that's not an option.

His mumbled reply is barely audible.

"Why don't you come by the apartment tonight? I could use the company and I can explain it better when I'm not sitting in a chair in the clerk's office at City Hall."

He reluctantly agrees and ends the call before I can offer any overzealous promises.

It's official. I'm the world's worst girlfriend. I have an amazing boyfriend who went out of his way to plan a romantic Valentine's getaway, and my ridiculous personal dramas have derailed our relationship—once again.

Maybe he would be better off without me. I'm kind of *a lot*. He needs someone less complicated. Someone more traditional. Someone who wants a big fancy wedding and a brood of little rugrats. A girl with a checkered past and a psychically unpredictable future probably isn't the best match for our hometown American hero.

Hold on. Am I talking myself into breaking up with Erick Harper on Valentine's Day?

Now I'm not just the world's worst girlfriend, I'm the world's worst—everything.

The clerk returns with two documents. She peers at me over the top of her reading glasses, and her gaze is not friendly. "These are the only birth certificates I was able to locate in the mother's married name."

"Great. Thank you." I shuffle the papers and wait for inspiration to strike. "Can you see if you have the mother's birth certificate? It says here the maiden name is Jankowski."

She continues to eye me over the rim of her tortoise-shell glasses. She's waiting expectantly for something.

It takes a moment to sink in, but I finally grab the pen and write Ania Jankowski on the notepad and push it toward her.

As soon as she walks out of sight, I snap pictures of the two birth certificates and slip my phone back in my pocket. Two children. Sons. Rajmund and Tadjo. The boys shouldn't be too hard to find, because their names will have remained the same. Fortunately there weren't any daughters. Tracking down marriage-related name changes would muddy the waters.

The clerk returns with another document and slides it across the counter. She pushes the note pad toward me. "In case you wanted to write down the names, dear."

Oh right. I'm supposed to pretend that I didn't take those pictures. Of course, that would mean I need notes. "Thank you. I will."

I write the names of the two Nowak children and add Ania Karina's birth date at the bottom of the list. "Do you know if any of the children remained in the area?"

She points toward the boys' certificates. "I think they all moved away. Right out of high school, if I remember correctly. Just disappeared one by one, you know?"

"Yes, I'm sure you're right." I take the two Nowak sons' birth certificates and push them toward her. "I'm finished with these, if you want to refile them."

She looks up, and for a moment I think she might have winked at me. She collects the two documents and returns to the back room.

I snap a quick photo of Ania Karina Jankowski's birth certificate, in case I need that info later, and hastily stow my phone.

When the clerk returns, I push the final birth certificate toward her. "Thank you very much for your help today."

She nods. "Good luck with your *project*, Miss Moon."

The way she says the word project shows she's probably on to my ruse. But as long as she's a willing participant, I won't complain. "Thank you," I call as I hustle out of City Hall.

Before my luck turns, I hurry back to the bookshop, hoping to catch Silas before he leaves.

No such luck. The bookstore is as empty as empty can be.

Grams, a hostage.

Twiggy, gone for the day.

Silas, heading home to his experiments, and Robin Pyewacket Goodfellow curled up in the lap of luxury in my father's penthouse across the alley.

Seems like the perfect time to have an extended pity party, but before I can throw myself into the role of wronged orphan a text pings on my phone. It's from Erick.

"Should I bring dinner?"

"Sure. You pick. About an hour?"

"K."

Yeesh! Never has one letter held so much information. If I'm going to have any hope of dragging this relationship back onto the rails, I better work a little harder in the "girlfriend" department.

Cut to—

Freshly showered Mitzy Moon, desperately seeking an appropriate outfit without the help of her fashion-diva Ghost-ma.

I grab the black skinny jeans and my super-cozy striped cashmere boyfriend sweater. It's an oldie, but a goodie. Now to create something hairstyle-adjacent, and go the extra mile with a slathering of makeup.

The eerie silence in the apartment is unnerving. I search for a party playlist on my phone and crank up the volume to drive away the *lack* of ghosts.

When all is said and done, even I have to admit I've made a solid effort.

Dancing my way out of the bathroom, I'm determined to boogie away my blues and make the best of my night with Erick.

BING. BONG. BING.

"He's here!" The missing echo of Grams' ethereal voice casts a shadow over my positive vibes.

Pausing beside the alleyway door, I catch my breath and paste on a disarming smile. "Good evening, Sheriff. Won't you come in?"

His worn-in-all-the-right-places jeans and casual button-down shirt show an effort that deserves to be acknowledged. "You look nice. I like that shirt."

He smiles, but the expression doesn't reach his eyes. "Thanks. You look nice too."

Oh boy! This is turning into a terrible first-date facsimile. "Why don't you head upstairs. I'll grab plates and stuff."

"K."

There it is again. That single letter doing the job of an entire soliloquy of disappointment. Come on, Moon. You got this.

Adding a couple cans of pop to the tower, I carefully make my way to the wrought-iron staircase. As you might've predicted, one of the cans rolls off when I attempt to climb over the "No Admittance" chain, and it bounces to the floor.

Embarrassment floods over me, and I snatch up the can and rush upstairs.

Of course, by the time I reach the apartment I'm not entirely sure which can is which.

Erick sets out the boxes from Myrtle's Diner,

and, despite my happiness at the sight of the golden french fries, the thought of my grandmother releases a cascade of tears.

He halts the setup and takes a seat next to me, but offers no comfort. "What's wrong now?"

"I deserve that. You have every right to be tired of the drama in my life. In fact, you have every right to a *way* better girlfriend. Someone who—"

His lips are on mine before I can finish my sentence.

The surge of love and tenderness that flows from that simple kiss erases all my excuses and nightmares.

He scoops me closer and tightens his arms around me.

The passionate kiss touches my heart and releases a fresh flood of tears. He tips my head back and wipes my tears with his thumb. "Don't ever say anything that foolish again. Okay?"

I nod and sniffle.

"And I think it's only fair to warn you, I'm not leaving this apartment until you tell me exactly what is going on with you, your grandmother's ghost, and this gypsy."

Dabbing my nose with the back of my hand, I nod. "That's fair. Let me clean myself up, and I'll tell you everything you want to know."

He slowly slides his hand from my side as I stand.

Before I make it two steps from the settee, a husky voice pierces the silence behind me. "I love you."

And there it is. The three little words that change everything.

This is absolutely one of the tropes that all the Rom-Coms get right. Time stands still.

In this case, though, I'm not sure if it's because the quicksand is sucking me under or because little cherubs in diapers are bearing me aloft.

I have to say something. Too much time is passing, and with each additional second of silence the impact of my reply increases exponentially.

I'm halfway through my achingly slow turn-around when Erick slides his arms around my waist. "Hey, you don't have to say anything. I'm not one of those guys with an ego made out of papier-mâché."

I nod and struggle to pull a small amount of air into my constricted chest.

He brushes a strand of hair from the side of my face and smiles that crooked smile that melts my heart and turns my legs to jelly. "I know my timing isn't great. But with the life I've lived and the things I saw on the battlefield, I think it's important to say what I feel when I feel it."

For some reason, his use of the word "battlefield" makes me giggle. I bite my lip to force the inappropriate silliness back into hiding.

His eyes widen. "Quick update: my ego is also not made out of titanium."

I wave my hands in surrender. "I'm sorry. I'm not laughing at you directly. It's just how my stupid brain works. When you said 'on the battlefield,' it brought up images of Civil War love stories in the Deep South, and it made me giggle."

He hugs me tight and kisses the tip of my nose. "And that's one of your many irresistible traits."

My head is filled with possible replies and a montage of "shoulds," but if my goal is to err on the side of honesty, there's only one thing I can say. "I'm in a weird place right now. I have way too much on my mind and way too many variables in getting my grandmother back safely."

He listens, and slowly slides his hand down my arm until he grips my fingers. "Go grab some tissues, and then you can fill me in on the details that were too top-secret for the telephone."

Nodding, I ease my hand from his, step into the bathroom, and wipe the smeared mascara from under my eyes. Bringing the tissue box back to the settee is probably a good idea.

"Let's dig into our food before it gets cold. My story's not going to get any better or worse because of a ten-minute delay."

He laughs out loud. "Ten minutes? Are you slowing down on me, Moon?"

"Rude."

We dig into our burgers and fries, and a scant five minutes later I'm wiping my mouth and preparing to spin my yarn.

He reaches for a soda, and, as he wiggles his finger under the tab, my accident on the circular staircase flashes to mind. "Wait!"

Too late. He chose poorly.

Soda sprays out of the can and all over his shirt. To his credit, his reflexes are remarkable, and he gets his mouth over the opening and shotguns the entire soft drink before a single drop hits my floor or the chair.

"Dude! That was impressive. I don't even want to know where you got those skills."

His eyes are watering and he waves a hand toward me as he chokes out the word, "Napkin."

I grab a handful and press them into his outstretched fingers. He wipes his face, dabs at his eyes, and makes a paltry attempt to soak some of the fizzy corn syrup from his shirt.

"Here, give me that shirt and I'll rinse it out in the sink. I can turn the heater on in the bathroom, and it should dry quickly."

It's not until he stands up and starts unbuttoning his shirt that the full effect of my offer dawns on me. Holy six pack! Erick is going to be shirtless in my apartment—for quite some time! For a split second, I'm almost grateful Grams isn't here to witness my serendipitous catastrophe.

He hands me the shirt, and his crooked grin is everything. "No rush."

My cheeks redden, and I hurry into the bathroom, shirt in hand, before I say anything I'll regret.

CHAPTER 20

I'M A GENUINE EXPERT at washing clothes in a bathroom sink. I shudder to think of the number of times I found myself without the requisite stacks of quarters required to use the sketchy pay-to-play laundry facilities in my rundown apartment.

Scrub, rinse, wring, shake out the wrinkles, and hang in front of the heater.

Closing the door behind me on my way out, I struggle to maintain my cool when I catch another glimpse of the shirtless sheriff. "It's not a very big room. It should heat up in there quick enough."

He walks toward me with the confidence of a jungle cat. "Like I said, no rush. Are you gonna tell me about this gypsy, or did you have something else planned?"

Oh brother! The way those jeans ride low on

his hips . . . I'm not sure how much more weak in the knees I can get without collapsing onto the floor. "I'd like to— When we— You sit."

Erick chuckles, clearly enjoying the power his semi-nakedness wields over me. He settles onto the couch and pats the cushion next to him.

With great effort, I attempt to ignore the rush of tingles bouncing around my body like a marble in a pinball machine and give him the highlights of my meeting with Mrs. Nowak and her terms of release.

"Did you have any luck tracking down the kids?"

"I know their names. Not sure how much that will help me, because the clerk said she thought they had all moved away. But I have a starting point with the two sons."

"What were the sons' names?"

"The oldest was Rajmund and the youngest Tadjo."

A flicker of recognition flashes across Erick's face. "What's the oldest boy's middle name?"

I flick to the image of the birth certificate on my phone and zoom in. "The birth record says, Rajmund Osburn Nowak."

Erick leans back and rubs his thumb along his jawline.

I'm mesmerized by the rise and fall of his broad chest.

"Moon, my eyes are up here." He points to his devilish blue-grey peepers.

Giggling with embarrassment, I playfully push him. The firm planes of his chest seem to trap my hand and I'm unable to withdraw.

He places his hand on top of mine and strokes his thumb along the back of my hand as he replies. "Have you considered the possibility that it's Ray Osborne at the hospital? He came into town about three years ago, if I remember correctly. No one seemed to know him, but he knew everything about the town. Isn't Nowak's husband named Osburn?"

There's no need to consult the images. As soon as Erick suggests the connection, my mood ring sizzles on my left hand. A casual glance reveals the face of Environmental Services manager Ray Osborne. I can instantly see the family resemblance. Now I'll have to cross my fingers and hope that he has a very poor memory for faces. Grams would know exactly what to wear to distract him from drawing any connection between the philanthropic Mizithra Moon and the temporary replacement janitor Darcy Brown.

Erick leans toward me and whispers hotly in my ear. "Where'd you go? How can I get you back?"

Oh, I'm back. I'm back and rapidly running out of oxygen. "Nothing. No one. I mean, I think I know Ray." I lean back and attempt a subtle gasp for air, and a quick subject change. "What are the odds he'd be open to a family reunion?"

"I've only had a couple conversations with him. We had to request 'no access' to a suspect's room last year and he coordinated with the cleaning crew. He seems like a decent guy. It can't hurt to ask."

"I'll take any slim chance of success I can get."

He smiles and looks deep into my eyes. "If we can get your grandmother back by Valentine's Day, will you promise to join me on the getaway?"

THUD. THUD. THUD. My heart feels as though it could beat straight out of my chest. "Um. Well..."

"It's a yes or no question, Moon." His smile is playful, but his eyes are pools of vulnerability.

"Yes. If Grams is back safe, then I'll feel better about taking off for the weekend."

He leans toward me and whispers a single word, "Deal." And then he seals that deal with a kiss.

As he slips his arms around me and the kiss continues, all I can picture is a high-stakes poker game where someone just pushed all their chips to the middle, and I have to either raise or fold.

I raise.

The time for all-night chat sessions or canoodling until the wee hours has passed. I'm going to take the risk.

I'm pushing in all my chips.

Leaning in to Erick's embrace, I allow my kiss to express my deepest feelings.

He leans back, and I follow, as though our hearts are bound together by an invisible thread. I feel the heat of his body through my sweater.

The sensation of cashmere slowly sliding upward fills me with anticipation.

CRASH!

In the blink of an eye, Erick is off the couch and pushing me protectively behind him. "Stay here." He reaches in the pocket of his coat and pulls out a small handgun.

Good to know. Even when he's sporting civilian clothes, my guy is still strapped up. And for those of you not addicted to real-crime TV, that means he's packing heat, or carrying a loaded weapon.

He presses the medallion by the secret door and waits for it to slide open, before slipping out and moving across the Rare Books Loft with the stealth of a—

"Don't shoot!" My extra senses deliver a shocking newsflash. "It's Pyewacket. It's only Pye! He must've accidentally knocked something over."

Erick flicks the safety on his gun and turns with a wry half grin. "Accidentally?"

I paint my features in a portrait of innocence and shrug. "What else could it be?"

He hooks his thumb in the waistband of his jeans and shakes his head. "I couldn't say, but I have my suspicions about that beast."

Pyewacket saunters across the mezzanine, and I swear that fiendish feline is wearing a smirk under his whiskers.

"Well, well, well. If it isn't Mr. Cuddlekins returning to subjugate yet another human."

Erick chuckles and puts his weapon back into the pocket of his coat.

I kneel and run my fingers along Pyewacket's spine. "Let's go see what mess you've made for me."

My half-naked boyfriend jogs into the bathroom and returns, buttoning up his shirt with a click of his tongue and a sigh that's more than mild disappointment. "I'll take the hint and head home for the night, Moon. But I think we made some real progress here."

He chuckles, and I blush beet red. "I'll let you know how things go with Ray tomorrow. Would it be all right if I drop your name, Sheriff?"

He zips his jacket, offers me a hand, and pulls me close for a goodnight kiss. "You can say anything you like as long as we get your grandmother home safe and sound."

It doesn't take a psychic to read the subtext of that message. "Copy that."

We walk hand-in-hand to the alleyway door,

and I offer him one last kiss before he disappears into the frosty February night.

Flipping on the lights, I peruse the first floor in search of Pyewacket's intrusive message.

Sure enough, he's knocked a book from the shelves. I stoop and retrieve it. *"Navigating the Healthcare System,* eh?"

"Ree-ooow!" His back arches in an unfriendly pose.

"Thanks, Pye. I definitely have to navigate something tomorrow. I'm not sure what drove Ray and his mother apart, but hopefully it's something that begging and/or money can fix."

I drop to the floor and sit cross-legged.

Pyewacket crawls into my lap and pushes his black-tufted ears against me.

"I miss her too. I miss her so much, it feels like there's a hole in my heart. I'm not sure how much longer I can be patient."

He nods his head as if he agrees.

"If this angle with the long-lost kids doesn't work, I'm afraid I'm gonna have to go rogue."

"REE-ow!" The sound of imminent retribution.

"I agree. We definitely can't tell Silas about our Plan B."

CHAPTER 21

WITHOUT THE GUIDING fashion wisdom of my grandmother, I'm left to my own devices in a confusing closet of couture.

In the end, I select a low-cut top, in the hopes that my cleavage will distract Mr. Osborne from taking notice of my face. Even though I take the easy way out by pairing it with skinny jeans, I force myself to choose a boot with a four-inch heel in honor of Grams.

"I'm off to save the day, Pyewacket. Are you going to wish me luck?"

He barely lifts his head from his perch amidst the depths of the down comforter. A soft growl is his only reply before he returns to kitty-cat dreamland.

Since today's visit is on the up and up, when I

reach the Birch County Regional Medical Facility, I enter through the front door and head straight to reception.

"Good morning. Mitzy Moon with the Duncan-Moon Philanthropic Foundation, here to see Mr. Osborne."

Might as well throw the cash around right out of the gate.

The receptionist obviously recognizes the name and quickly picks up the phone to call Ray.

Smiling pleasantly, I glance around the waiting room and ask myself why so many hospitals think pale-green is an attractive color.

"Mr. Osborne said to send you right down. Do you need a map?"

"I'm sure I can find it. Just point me in the direction I need to go."

She places a map of the facility on the counter. "Reception is here, and Environmental Services is back here. If you head down that hallway—"

"Thank you so much." A little too sing-songy, but pretending I don't know where I'm going is already boring me to death. I strut down the corridor and rehearse my speech as I go.

Having lost my mother at such a young age, I would do anything to have her back. It's a little hard for me to understand what could drive a child away from a parent so completely. But I'm not here to pass judgment on Ray. I'm here to see if there is anything, in all of Christendom, I can do to bring him into the same room with his dying mother.

Fingers crossed. Accepting any and all help from the universe.

Before entering the Environmental Services manager's office, for the second time, I take a deep breath and paste on an enormous fake smile.

"Good morning, Mr. Osborne." The false jubilant tone rings hollow in my ears, but seems to do the trick with my mark.

Ray Osborne, a.k.a. Rajmund Osburn Nowak, looks away from his computer screen and barely manages a smile. "How can I help you, Miss Moon?"

I carefully drop into one of the dusty-rose vinyl-covered chairs in front of his desk and cross my arms under my bosom in hopes of enhancing my assets.

He continues to stare directly at my face—unblinkingly. He has zero interest in my wares.

Here goes nothing. "Mr. Osborne, I am actually not here on behalf of the foundation. However, if there is anything that we can do for your department, I hope you'll let me know. My visit this morning is of a personal nature."

His energy shifts immediately. My clairsentience picks up on a hint of fear with a side of irritation. "As I'm sure you can imagine, Miss Moon, running a medical facility this size requires my complete focus. I'm afraid I don't know you, and I'm certain we don't have any personal business to discuss."

Well, he asked for it. No more beating around the bush. "Mr. *Nowak*, I'm here to discuss your mother."

His eyes widen, and he pushes back from his desk. His arms cross over his chest and my clairaudience distinctly hears the word "run."

"I know you came back to town about three years ago with a new name and no intention of letting your parents know you'd returned. I'm not here to out you or cause you any personal problems. Your mother has something of mine, and her condition to return it to me is that I facilitate a meeting with her children."

Rather than reducing his defiant posture and uncooperative energy, my statement seems to cause his resistance to deepen.

"Ray . . . May I call you Ray?"

He does not respond.

"Your mother is dying. I have no idea what happened to you and your brother to cause such a rift between you and your parents—"

"Just her."

Interesting. "I'm sorry, between you and your

mother, but I'm desperate to get back what she took from me."

His arms loosen slightly, and his jaw flinches. "Aren't they all."

"What do you mean?"

"You want to know what happened, growing up with that witch for a mother? I'll tell you. Every person in this town had something against us. Her quack potions or her spells gone wrong. My brother and I were the butt of endless Polack jokes at school, not to mention every possible form of witch hunt. I can't even begin to count the number of times there were dead animals or bowls of pig's blood in my locker."

A sick feeling twists in my gut. "I'm so sorry. Why dead animals?"

He leans forward and looks at me as though I'm an idiot. "Don't you know anything about witch-craft? People always think it's Satan worship and animal sacrifice. It's none of those things. My brother and I had no interest in the craft, and we certainly didn't have any interest in educating a backward population." The anger and vehemence in his words are as fresh as if the wounds were inflicted yesterday.

"Ray, I'm truly sorry. I know how cruel children can be. I grew up in the foster system, and there may not be as many Orphan Annie jokes as there are witch trials, but it was no picnic."

His energy softens, and his hands fall to his lap.

We're not friends, but at least there's a faint thread of connection. Nothing like childhood trauma to create a bond. "I'm going to go out on a limb and tell you the truth. Your mother stole my grandmother's ghost. My grandmother has been trapped on this side of the veil since she crossed over, and she and I have been building a posthumous relationship that we never had the opportunity to forge when she was alive. She's practically the most important thing in the world to me, and your mother took her, to force me—"

He exhales loudly and hangs his head. "Say no more. The truth is, I know all about her illness. It's the reason I came back. My father told me about episodes she'd been having and her refusal to get any treatment, because of the cost." He takes a deep breath and rubs a hand along his receding hairline. "I changed my name years ago, right after I left home. So it was easy to come back here with my résumé and pretend I had no connection to the community. I was overqualified for this job, and they gave it to me in a heartbeat. I set up a shell company to pay a portion of her medical bills without her knowing. I don't want a relationship with her, Miss Moon. But I also didn't want my father to have to watch her suffer or drown under a mountain of bills."

"Ray, I don't have anything to offer you beyond money, and you don't seem like the kind of guy who is open to bribery. But I need you to call your brother and promise me that you'll meet with her. I have to get my grandmother back. Please, please help me."

The tense muscles along his jaw relax and the lines around his eyes fade as I feel his energy shift toward cooperation. "My brother is a tough nut to crack."

"I'm happy to call him with you right now. Maybe if he understands how desperate I am, he'll take the chance."

Ray chews his bottom lip and shakes his head. "I don't know. He chose a lifestyle she wouldn't approve of."

"What do you mean?"

He rubs his hands together and rests them on his desk. "I'm not sure if it's my place to say." There's an uncomfortable pause and his eyes dart left and right. "He's in the theater. She wanted him to be a lawyer. Said he always had the smarts for it, and he got top marks. Probably could've gotten a scholarship anywhere. But the second he graduated, he loaded everything in a car and headed for New York. He eked out a living on the boards for years, before he found his path as a director."

For the first time since I walked through the door, a tinge of happiness filters through Ray's aura.

"He's doing all right for himself."

Leaning forward, I take a chance and place my hand on top of Ray's. "My grandmother means everything to me. Will you please call him?"

He pulls out his cell phone, taps a number on his speed dial, and places it on speaker. "Tadjo, do you have a minute?"

"Always for you, big brother."

Ray looks at me and shrugs. "Full disclosure, I'm here on speakerphone and there's a woman in my office named Mitzy Moon."

Tadjo's light laughter filters through the phone. "Are you finally going to tie the knot, bro?"

Ray shakes his head and chuckles. "Confirmed bachelor. One divorce is enough for me. She's actually—" Ray looks at me helplessly.

"Hi Tadjo. I'm gonna jump into this headfirst and I hope you'll forgive me later. I've been living with the ghost of my grandmother for more than a year. A couple of days ago your mother ghostnapped my grandma, and as ransom she's demanding a meeting with you and your brother."

Bitter laughter, followed by whooping and hollering, surprises me. "Some things never change, eh,

Ray? Look, miss, I left that town thirty years ago, and I've never looked back. What makes you think I'd drag myself back there for some woman I've never met with a story as ludicrous as yours?"

Two things I know about Broadway: it's very expensive to put on a show; and you're only as good as your last review. Advantage Moon. "I tell you what, Tadjo, you come back here and do me this favor, and I'll make sure your next production is fully funded before the script is finished."

Silence.

My extrasensory perception picks up on the fact that it's an awestruck moment of quiet, rather than non-responsiveness. "I must've failed to mention, my grandmother was Isadora Duncan."

Tadjo gasps. "My, my, my! So that funding promise is no joke?"

"I don't joke about money, Mr. Nowak."

Ray and I exchange a glance and sit in silence, waiting for Tadjo's reply.

"As it happens, I'm in between shows right now. I can be on a plane this afternoon. But I'm booking my return flight for tomorrow. Set up the meeting for tonight, and be sure to let Ania know this is a one-time thing, and I have no plans to stay in town."

"Acceptable terms. I'll set up the meeting for 7:00 p.m." I glance at Ray and raise my eyebrows questioningly.

"Works for me. I'll pick you up at the airport, Tadjo. Text me when your plane lands."

The Broadway director clears his throat and sings his next line. "Hold on to your cherries kids, Broadway's coming to town."

Visions of "jazz hands" dance in my head.

CHAPTER 22

THE MEETING IS SET. Ray and Tadjo are going to meet us in the parking lot outside the emporium. Silas is coming with me in case Grams needs some type of alchemical triage after we make the exchange.

The day's half-frozen sleet left a coating of treacherous ice on the roads. Even if the roads were clear, I think I'd still be driving slowly. The weight of the handgun tucked in my jeans and pressing against my spine has me on edge.

Don't worry, I'm not planning to kill anyone. But I promised Pyewacket I'd have a Plan B, and if this gypsy doesn't hold up her end of the bargain, I will do whatever it takes to get my grandmother back.

Despite my slow rate of travel, we're the first to

arrive. I leave the engine running to keep warm as long as possible.

"I shall require you to pass me the gun, at once."

"How did you— I mean, what gun?"

Silas ignores my attempt at a cover-up and calmly holds his open palm in front of me.

Exhaling in frustration, I lean forward and slide the gun out of my waistband. "Here. But don't blame me if things go sideways in there and we're left without a back-up plan."

He chuckles to himself as he checks the gun's safety catch and places the firearm in the glove box.

"What do we do if she reneges on the deal?"

"Are you concerned the boys were engaged in subterfuge? Do you feel they will not arrive?"

"No. I got the feeling they were legit. I just don't think it's going to be some sappy holiday-movie reunion. Neither of them wants anything to do with their mother. If she's expecting an other-worldly mending of hearts, I'm worried she'll be disappointed."

Silas smooths his mustache and nods. "And you fear this disappointment will lead to further blackmail?"

"Exactly. The gun was my insurance policy. Shoot some stuff up, cause a distraction, and grab the amulet."

"The situation is not like one of your movies,

Mizithra. Shooting things up to cause a distraction could end badly. Far worse than you imagine. If Mrs. Nowak does not honor our bargain, I am prepared to take extreme measures."

An odd chill ripples from the top of my skull, across my shoulders. I'm not sure I want to find out what it's like to disappoint Mr. Willoughby in such important matters. "Copy that."

Another vehicle pulls into the parking lot and two men step out.

Silas and I exit the Jeep and walk toward them.

Waving hesitantly at Ray, I'm both shocked and pleased when I take in all that is Tadjo. He's everything I'd imagined. Sophistication ensconced in a luxuriously long scarf, his head tucked snugly into a slouchy beanie, and his designer coat screaming New York. In a word—fabulous! I offer my hand. "I'm Mitzy Moon."

He grips my outstretched hand, and the buttery leather of his kidskin gloves caresses my fingers. "Well, aren't you a dream! I can't promise you this tête-à-tête is going to give you the results you want, darling, but I'm here to give the performance of a lifetime." He drops my hand and flourishes his arm as he strikes a pose.

Perhaps Ray's statement about Tadjo being "in theater" was a code phrase for his brother's obviously flamboyant lifestyle. No judgment. But there could be more at play between the younger brother and the matriarch than a failure to attend law school.

Silas and I enter the emporium first. When I see Mrs. Nowak in an old chair with a hand-knitted afghan covering her legs, I almost fall prey to her deception.

Silas whispers softly in my right ear. "Perhaps Tadjo is not the only one giving the performance of a lifetime."

I bite my tongue sharply to prevent an outburst of laughter, but Silas is not wrong.

"Mrs. Nowak, your sons have agreed to meet with you as a one-time-only favor to me. Now, I'd like to collect my grandmother and leave."

A flash of amber in her lap catches the light. "Not so fast, girly. Where are my boys?"

Turning to take in the empty space behind me, I hustle back to the door and motion for them to come in. Neither of them is in any hurry.

The moment they enter, she gasps and clutches her chest. Tears spring to her eyes as she stares wordlessly at her sons.

Tadjo is the first to find his voice. "Good evening, mother. I'm catching a plane home tomorrow, so you should know that whatever nonsense you have planned with this one-woman show, it won't be getting an encore." He swishes his scarf over his shoulder and places his hands on his hips defiantly.

Ray is less dramatic and more direct. "The only reason we're here, Mrs. Nowak, is to prevent you from ruining yet another life. You don't get to control us anymore, and this is not a reconciliation. You stole something from Miss Moon. We're here to see that you give it back. That is all."

Her tears vanish, and the invalid's throw falls to the shabby carpet as she gets to her feet. "Thankless children. After everything I did for you."

Oh dear! This is headed south rapidly.

A voice drifts through the ether. "I hope you and Silas have an exit strategy, dear. She's been lining up spells all day to try and trap her sons here and bind them to her somehow. You've got to get that book away from her! She's a dangerous woman, with horrible plans."

Understood, Grams.

I whisper the SparkNotes version to Silas and feel power swirl around him.

He steps forward. "Mrs. Nowak, we will be taking the amulet and *Loca Sine Lumine, Loca Sine Lege.* Delving into powers not meant for you is what has led to your severe illness—"

Tadjo pushes past Silas and strides closer to his mother. "Illness? No one said anything about an illness. Are you dying? Has your obsession with dark magicks finally robbed you of your life?"

His words are grandiose, but my heart feels the pain of a young son who may lose his mother far sooner than he imagined.

Ray slips past me, places a hand on his brother's arm, and attempts to pull him toward the exit. "Come on, T. The illness was bound to happen someday."

Tadjo shakes his brother's hand off his arm and stands toe to toe with his mother. "All these years, trying to wield power you had no business with, and now this? You've taken this poor girl's grandmother?" He weeps openly.

My extra senses confirm that his performance is only ten percent authentic. She reaches for him, and he steps back in horror. "You can't rebuild a relationship with your own family by destroying someone else's." He turns with a flourish and crosses his arms.

"Mitzy, can you hear me?"

Quick thought message to Grams. *Loud and clear.*

"The book is behind the counter. There's a secret panel in the kick plate, near the register."

I send a mental picture of the book to Silas, and he nods once.

Stepping behind the counter, I drop to all fours and let my psychic senses guide me to the panel.

"What is happening? Where did she go?" The concern and panic in the gypsy's voice are not an act.

Silas replies without hesitation. "You made a bargain. And we are here to collect."

My fingers tingle and I press the panel. It pops open and I grab the book. "Got it!"

As my head surfaces above the counter, several things happen simultaneously.

Silas reaches his hand forward, and the amulet struggles to answer the call.

The gypsy holds the chain and fights the commanding force of my mentor.

Tadjo steps between his mother and the alchemist, and yanks the amulet from his mother's hands. He drops it into Silas's outstretched palm. "This is your last chance, mother. Let these people leave in peace, or you will never see me again. You will die alone and unloved. No less than you deserve."

I hustle toward the door, and Silas turns to join me.

Ray nods to us, and I mouth a "thank you" in his direction.

Energy snaps and crackles inside the emporium, and I glance over my shoulder in time to see the wooden table with the display of tarot cards explode into pieces.

Rajmund shields his brother from the debris, and Mrs. Nowak sobs as her sons turn to leave.

Silas grips my elbow and moves me purposefully across the icy parking lot. The slick surface seems to melt beneath our feet, and I wonder what transmutation creates this safe passage.

Risking one more glance as we exit the parking lot, I note the boys are still inside. Perhaps they will find a way to call a truce with their mother, but, in all honesty, I don't care.

I got my grandmother back, and, right now, nothing else in the world matters.

Well, possibly one thing . . .

Successful grandmother recovery = Valentine's overnight getaway with Erick.

Gulp!

CHAPTER 23

SILAS PROMISES to return first thing in the morning and use his wealth of arcane knowledge to release Grams from the amulet and put everything right in our world.

Meanwhile, I have a phone call to make. Laying the amulet on the four-poster bed next to Pye, I promise to return as soon as I update Erick.

"Be careful with Ghost-ma while I'm gone, Pyewacket." Addressing the amulet, I add, "I'll be back in a flash."

Out to the mezzanine, with a thin veil of privacy, I blurt out my exciting news the second Erick answers the phone.

A soft groan wasn't the response I was expecting.

"What's wrong? I thought that was our deal? I get Grams back and off we go."

He explains how the fates have sabotaged our Valentine's getaway. His mother slipped on a dangerous patch of ice in the driveway, returning from the mailbox, and broke her wrist. He's currently in the emergency room and will be spending his Valentine's weekend playing nursemaid to his injured mother.

I have to chuckle. Not about his mother's injury, but definitely in regard to my love life. "It really wasn't meant to be. You take care of your mom, and I'll try to bring Isadora up to speed on everything she missed. We'll have another opportunity for a getaway." My tummy tingles and my heart pitter-patters, when he promises to make good on our "deal."

"All right, Grams, I'm all yours."

"No Valentine's plans with your yummy sheriff?"

"Um, no, and I'm not sure I like you referring to him as yummy." I scoop the pendant from the bed, carry it into the closet, and hang Grams on a hook. Over the next several hours, I take her through a wardrobe recap of everything she missed.

My attempt to skip over the details of my evening with Erick, and the cashmere boyfriend sweater, fails miserably. I'm forced to tell her every sordid detail about the splattered soda and the shirt-less sheriff.

When the thin grey light of morning interrupts my update, my body finally admits defeat. "Grams, I've gotta catch a little shuteye. Where would you like me to leave you?"

"Just leave me in here, dear. Next to you, these are the things I love the most."

After an intense three-hour power nap, the voice of Silas Willoughby crackles over the intercom.

"Good morning, Mizithra. I hope you are decent. I must speak with you."

Sleep deprived and more than a little punchy, I roll out of bed with a case of the giggles. "Did you hear that, Grams?"

She adds her tinkling laughter to mine. "That man could make a dessert menu sound like an end-of-days catastrophe!"

Searching the floor, I find my robe and make myself *decent*.

The bookcase door slides open, and my regular and extra senses take a simultaneous shot to the gut. "What's wrong? It's bad, isn't it?"

He shuffles toward the scalloped-back chair, and his jowls seem to sag more than normal. Silas collapses into the chair and adjusts his tattered tweed coat. His entire being emanates defeat.

"Silas? What's going on?"

"Mitzy! Don't leave me hanging." Ghost-ma calls from the closet.

Grams and I burst out laughing at her clever pun.

Silas moans and shakes his head. While he fishes something out of his fusty old coat, I step into the closet and retrieve my grandma-in-a-stone.

Placing the pendant on the coffee table, I take a seat. "Are you ready to break her out of this amber prison?"

Silas moans a second time, and this one sounds like a wounded animal.

"He needs to get over himself, Mitzy. If he has bad news, tell him to spill it."

Taking a quick stint as an afterlife interpreter, I share her message.

The weary alchemist smooths his mustache and draws a slow breath. "I have delved into every tome I possess on the topic. I fear we find ourselves in the very worst of a Catch 22."

"How's that now?"

"When the gypsy trapped your grandmother in the amulet, she wielded powers beyond her understanding. She successfully severed the tie that bound Isadora to this bookshop. Hence the ability to trap her ghost in the stone and remove her from the property."

Grams snickers. "Tell us something we don't know."

I chew the inside of my cheek and stifle any bubbling silliness. "All right. That seems obvious. What about the spe— transmutation, to release Ghost-ma from this stupid necklace?"

He clicks his tongue and exhales. "And that is where we reach the impasse. I have already been to the emporium this morning. On that front, I do have a bit of good news. Tadjo canceled his return flight to New York and has chosen to stay with his mother during her last days. Your efforts were not wasted. Healing has begun."

"That's good, right?"

"Indeed. Mrs. Nowak was in a fine mood, and allowed me to persuade her to give me a peek at her mother's grimoire. Sadly, the notes provided no solution of which I was not already aware."

Smiling hopefully, I lean toward my mentor. "Solution seems like a positive word."

"Forgive me. I misspoke. Possible solution. The issue I cannot solve is the one that cuts the deepest. I have found at least three possible ways to release Isadora's ghost from imprisonment. The issue—"

"That's great!" Grams and I shout in unison.

"The issue becomes the event that transpires immediately following the release."

"What's he talking about? Ask him what he's

talking about, dear."

"She wants to know what you mean?"

A dark cloud seems to pass over him and his gaze drops to the floor. "The tether we implanted before her death has been broken. If I release Isadora from the amulet, I have uncovered no way to keep her from crossing over."

A dreadful silence floods the apartment.

Staring at the pendant as though it's a coiled rattlesnake ready to strike, I've never felt more helpless. "So what do we do? How do we get her out of *there* but keep her in *here*?"

Silas shakes his head and wipes a small tear from the wrinkled corner of his eye. "We cannot. If you choose to release her, we will lose her forever. For now, we must keep her in the amber while I continue my research. There are a few trusted souls I may contact for help, but you and your grandmother must face the truth. She may never be free to roam this bookstore again."

Grams started crying several sentences ago, but I caged my emotions in hopes that there would be a happy ending to his story. Now my tears flow freely, and Pyewacket hurries over to comfort me.

"I don't want to lose you, Grams. It's not fair for me to make the decision, though. Staying, just to be trapped in that stupid necklace—it's too much to ask. What do you want?"

She's sobbing and sniffling, and I can picture the sparkling tears streaming down her ethereal face. "Of course I choose to stay with you, sweetie. I'd rather be trapped in a piece of amber than on the other side of the veil without you. Have faith. Silas will find a way. For now, nothing has changed. We can still talk, and laugh, and I can tell you what to wear."

Smiling through my tears, I share her decision with Silas.

"Very well. I must return home and rest. I was at the books all night. I will not give up the search, but I shall not make empty promises. If at any point you change your mind, Isadora, I will be here to release you."

I pass along her thanks, and Silas takes his leave.

My grumbling stomach echoes in the silence. "I need to grab some breakfast at the diner. I'll be back before you know it." I stumble toward the closet to grab jeans and a sweater.

"Take me with you!"

"Isadora, you know you're tethered—" Wait! She's not tethered. She's free as a bird. As long as her ghost is trapped in that amulet, she can go anywhere she likes. I mean, I can take her anywhere she likes.

"I can't wait to see Odell!"

"Look, just because your circumstances have changed, doesn't mean our rules have. No thought-dropping!" My attempt at a stern warning fails miserably as my excitement builds.

She giggles when I secure the pendant's chain around my neck.

The warmth of the diner is more welcoming today than it has ever been. I stomp the dirty slush off my shoes and walk across the black-and-white checkered floor with a spring in my step.

Tally places a cup of coffee on the table and winks. The diner is bustling, and she doesn't have time for chitchat.

"My goodness, that woman looks younger now than last time I saw her. Hard work does a body good."

I bite my lower lip to prevent myself from blurting my reply out loud. *Easy, Grams. I don't want to mess up in public. All right?*

"10-4. And I'm saluting. Since you can't see me, I thought I'd give you the play-by-play."

Please, spare me.

Odell approaches the table, and his eyes immediately fall on the pendant. "That's a beautiful necklace, Mitzy. Seems like it sparkles from the inside."

I can hear Grams crying softly and force myself

to ignore it. "Thanks. It's really special. Glad you like it. Maybe I'll wear it more often."

He pushes my breakfast toward me, raps his knuckles twice on the table, and returns to the kitchen.

"Oh Mitzy, I miss him terribly."

Her passion for her first husband reminds me of the pilfered medical files. Fast as lightning, I force myself to think of anything else. Stellen and Yolo enjoying their Valentine's dinner. Pyewacket pushing a book off the shelf.

"What's going on? What medical records?"

My guilt flashes like a neon sign in my consciousness, and she easily reads the message. The inappropriate review of her private medical records is now public knowledge—at least between the two of us. *I'm sorry. I wanted to tell you. I mean, I didn't plan to tell you right now, over breakfast, but I was going to tell you. I'm sorry that I invaded your privacy. I'm also really sorry about the baby you lost. That must've been hard for you and Odell. You love my dad so much, and you're a wonderful mother— but you're an even better grandmother. Can you forgive me?*

Sniffling is interrupted by a ragged sigh. "It was all too much for me. The fights between Odell and Cal, losing the baby. I had to run away. Then I made a lot of bad choices with my second husband. I loved Max, in my own way, but I never got over Odell. Don't get me wrong, my years with Cal and raising your father are still some of the happiest memories I have, but Odell was my first love. True love never leaves you. Do you know what I mean?"

The door opens and a gust of brisk air blows in a handsome sheriff in civilian clothes.

Tally walks toward him with a perfectly packaged to-go order.

He hands her some cash and catches sight of me just in time. Striding to my booth, he leans down, and, right as he's about to kiss me, the amulet stops him in his tracks. "Is that your grandmother?" he whispers.

"Shhhh. I'm having enough trouble keeping her in line. I don't need you jumping on her bandwagon."

"Kiss him, Mitzy. Be in the moment! Don't miss an opportunity like this."

Not sure whether my actions are under my own control, I lean forward and firmly kiss Erick Harper's pouty mouth. "I'm sorry we had to cancel our plans. I hope your mother's feeling better. You'll give her my best, won't you?"

His warm smile sends a flash of heat through my body. "I will." The next kiss lingers longer than appropriate in public, and I sense a distraction.

When he finally pulls away, there's a mischievous grin on his face, and he winks as he turns to leave.

Don't get me wrong, I could watch this man walk away all day long. However, as the door closes behind him and my attention returns to the table, I'm greeted by the charming homemade Valentine that he slipped under the edge of my plate while his luscious lips distracted me.

Grams is crying again. "He's the sweetest man! What is it they say? Lock that down? You need to lock that down, Mitzy."

I chuckle into my napkin and beg her to be quiet while I read the card's sentiment:

Dear Mitzy,
    Fate only counts if you let it. You and I are destined to be.
    No rush. No worries. Our future is forever.
    Love, Erick.

Grams gasps, and I can picture her clutching her pearls.

It might not be a typical Valentine's Day, but it's definitely the best one I've ever had.

End of Book 12

A NOTE FROM TRIXIE

Should we get Stellen and Yolo their own series? Another case solved! I'll keep writing them if you keep reading . . .

The best part of "living" in Pin Cherry Harbor continues to be feedback from my early readers. Thank you to my alpha readers/cheerleaders, Angel and Michael. HUGE thanks to my fantastic beta readers who continue to give me extremely useful and honest feedback: Veronica McIntyre and Nadine Peterse-Vrijhof. And big "small town" hugs to the world's best ARC Team – Trixie's Mystery ARC Detectives!

All hail my long-suffering editor, Philip Newey. Thank you for continuing to help me understand the power of the comma. I'd also like to give mad props to Brooke for her tireless proofreading! Any errors are my own, as my outdated version of Word insists on showing me only what it likes and when it feels so moved.

Shout out to H. Claire Taylor for an intense story session that helped me refine this adventure and flesh out new characters.

FUN FACT: Once upon a time, I worked as a custodian in a high-rise office building!

My favorite quote from this case: "I wish I could tell you that I was able to stop myself from rolling my eyes, but I can't." ~ Mitzy

I'm currently writing book fourteen in the Mitzy Moon Mysteries series, and I think I may just live in Pin Cherry Harbor forever. Mitzy, Grams, and Pyewacket got into plenty of trouble in book one, *Fries and Alibis*. But I'd have to say that book three, *Wings and Broken Things*, is when most readers say the series becomes unputdownable.

I hope you'll continue to hang out with us.

Trixie Silvertale (February 2021)

Mitzy Moon Mysteries 13

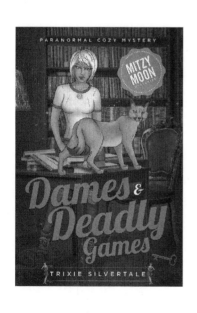

A murder mystery game. A terminal twist. Can this psychic sleuth swap coal for clues?

Mitzy Moon hopes to earn some girlfriend points on a scenic weekend getaway. Steaming off on a historic train with her handsome beau seems like the perfect way to outrun fate. But their 1920s-themed sleuthing party abruptly derails when they discover an actual corpse . . .

Now they're on the wrong side of the tracks, and Mitzy and her sheriff will have to solve the case before the guilty party disappears at the next depot. With a list of suspects as long as the cast of characters, she'll need to push her powers to the boiling point before more tickets get lethally punched.

Will Mitzy's dangerous excursion end with an arrest, or will the killer claim another life?

Dames and Deadly Games is the thirteenth book in the hilarious paranormal cozy mystery series, Mitzy Moon Mysteries. If you like snarky heroines, supernatural misfits, and a dash of romance, then you'll love Trixie Silvertale's iron horse escapade.

Buy *Dames and Deadly Games* to blow the whistle on a murderer today!

Grab yours here!
readerlinks.com/l/1671623

Scan this QR Code with the camera on your phone. You'll be taken right to the Mitzy Moon Mysteries series page. You can easily grab any mysteries you've missed!

Once you're in the Club, you'll also be the first to receive

updates from Pin Cherry Harbor and access to giveaways, new release announcements, behind-the-scenes secrets, and much more!

Scan this QR Code with the camera on your phone. You'll be taken right to the page to join the Club!

THANK YOU!

Trying out a new book is always a risk and I'm thankful that you rolled the dice with Mitzy Moon. If you loved the book, the sweetest thing you can do (*even sweeter than pin cherry pie à la mode*) is to leave a review so that other readers will take a chance on Mitzy and the gang.

Don't feel you have to write a book report. A brief comment like, "Can't wait to read the next book in this series!" will help potential readers make their choice.

★★★★★
Leave a quick review HERE
https://readerlinks.com/l/1596178
★★★★★

Thank you kindly, and I'll see you in Pin Cherry Harbor!

ABOUT THE AUTHOR

Trixie Silvertale grew up reading an endless supply of Lilian Jackson Braun, Hardy Boys, and Nancy Drew novels. She loves the amateur sleuths in cozy mysteries and obsesses about all things paranormal. Those two passions unite in her Mitzy Moon Mysteries, and she's thrilled to write them and share them with you.

When she's not consumed by writing, she bakes to fuel her creative engine and pulls weeds in her herb garden to clear her head (*and sometimes she pulls out her hair, but mostly weeds*).

Greetings are welcome:
trixie@trixiesilvertale.com

BB bookbub.com/authors/trixie-silvertale

f facebook.com/TrixieSilvertale

O instagram.com/trixiesilvertale

Printed in Great Britain
by Amazon

66110280R00168